WISDOM *in the*
Telling

WISDOM in the Telling

Finding Inspiration and Grace in Traditional Folktales and Myths Retold

Lorraine Hartin-Gelardi

Walking Together, Finding the Way®
SKYLIGHT PATHS®
PUBLISHING
Woodstock, Vermont

Wisdom in the Telling:
Finding Inspiration and Grace in Traditional Folktales and Myths Retold

2006 First Printing
© 2006 by Lorraine Hartin-Gelardi

See pp. 171–174 for a continuation of this copyright page.

Library of Congress Cataloging-in-Publication Data
Hartin-Gelardi, Lorraine, 1955–
    Wisdom in the telling : finding inspiration and grace in traditional folktales and myths retold / Lorraine Hartin-Gelardi.
        p. cm.
    Includes bibliographical references.
    ISBN-13: 978-1-59473-185-3
    ISBN-10: 1-59473-185-3
    1. Tales. 2. Legends. 3. Oral tradition. 4. Storytelling. 5. Communication in folklore. I. Title.

GR73.H37 2006
398.2—dc22

2006022335

10 9 8 7 6 5 4 3 2 1

Manufactured in the United States of America
Jacket Design: Sara Dismukes

SkyLight Paths Publishing is creating a place where people of different spiritual traditions come together for challenge and inspiration, a place where we can help each other understand the mystery that lies at the heart of our existence.

SkyLight Paths sees both believers and seekers as a community that increasingly transcends traditional boundaries of religion and denomination—people wanting to learn from each other, *walking together, finding the way.*

Walking Together, Finding the Way®
Published by SkyLight Paths Publishing
A Division of Longhill Partners, Inc.
Sunset Farm Offices, Route 4, P.O. Box 237
Woodstock, VT 05091
Tel: (802) 457-4000   Fax: (802) 457-4004
www.skylightpaths.com

For Meghan, Kevin, and Brendan,
whose stories I hold
within my heart

CONTENTS

INTRODUCTION

We are cradled in a web of stories that holds us fast, encircling us with the intricate strands of humankind's history, connecting the thread of our own lives to this multifaceted tangle of tales. Through a story, we enter a world beyond time and place, a world made up of incredible characters and improbable occurrences. This world captures our imagination, stirs up our emotions, and we find that the images in the story remain with us long after the tale has ended. The story encourages us to look inward and explore the hidden terrain of our heart. We discover aspects of ourselves mirrored in these tales and realize that we are not alone. We find wisdom, grace, and inspiration in these tales to connect us to all that is human and all that is divine, to all that is true in the world.

Our trials and tribulations, our deepest longings, our triumphs are echoed in these ancient tales, which have traveled across the boundaries of culture and geography, reminding us that we share a universal human experience. The stories that we internalize shape our lives. They color the way we see our world and give meaning to our individual experiences, allowing us to understand who we are and helping us to find our place in the world. We communicate these stories in many ways. We weave our personal observations and the anecdotes of our lives in with these familiar tales as a way of breaking down barriers between strangers and offering the hand of friendship. We reveal our most intimate feelings to those we love by sharing the tales that have touched us deeply. We impart the wisdom we have found in our stories by passing them from one generation to the next.

I am a storyteller and my repertoire involves a wide assortment of tales, including personal stories, humorous anecdotes, historical narratives, and literary tales. I especially enjoy telling myths and folktales. Myths attempt to explain the origins of the world and offer profound insights into the human psyche. Folktales are traditional narratives found in every culture, each group adding its particular interpretation of the human condition to the collective wisdom. When I share my rendition of these tales, I add my voice to the chorus of the human story. Some of the stories in this collection I have told for many years; others are relatively new. All have settled into the landscape of my mind, accompanying me as I travel through life. They offer guidance, shedding new light on old memories, shaping the way I perceive my experiences, and helping me cope with difficult situations. As I continue to share them, they reveal new layers of meaning and deeper levels of authenticity.

As a storyteller, I become the medium for the story, creating a picture with words and enhancing those words with tone of voice, rhythm, facial expression, and body gesture to make the story come alive and let listeners see it in their imaginations. Committing these stories to the written page required me to shift my use of language and gave me an opportunity to expand and broaden the stories. In writing these stories, I experimented with a technique that I learned from storyteller and author Doug Lipman called *image riding*, a process that encourages images to bubble up from deep inside the mind and freely enter the imagination. This "wide-awake dreaming" allowed me to see the stories in a new way. All the stories gathered in this volume are original retellings of the old tales. In some cases, I combined several versions of a myth or folktale to produce a unique rendering of the story. At other times, I appreciably altered a single tale. Despite the outward changes, the essence of the old story remains.

Throughout the ages, people of various cultures and faith traditions have handed down wisdom through stories. The world of the imagination is the territory where stories unfold, kindling our sense of wonder and awakening our spirit. Stories are not to be taken at face value; their otherworldly quality begs us to look anew at our ordinary world. The wondrous elements in the story are symbolic. They point us toward the mystery that is at the core of our own lives, leading us out of the everyday and connecting us to the timeless. The heroes and heroines in some of the tales enter incredible worlds and receive help from magical creatures and talismans. However, they do not remain in those worlds. Instead, they return to their regular lives, transformed by their encounters. The stories present us with similar gifts, strengthening and enlightening us, offering us insights into our daily lives.

The stories in this collection touch on the unchanging concerns of the human heart. While each story deals with a specific theme, it also contains several aspects of a larger truth. These various aspects of the truth are often echoed in other stories, expressing a collective body of wisdom. As human beings, one of our deepest needs is to connect with others—to be understood and loved within our families, and to develop the bonds of community. Sharing our stories—listening to one another—enables us to establish these connections. A number of the stories in this volume express the way in which we try to do this. We determine our family identity by what we choose to remember as well as what we choose to forget. Often our memories keep us mired in the past and prevent us from forgiving those who have hurt us. Healing takes place when we understand what has happened in the past. The stories also reflect the generous nature of the universe, allowing us to see the wonder of the world around us and teaching us how to respond to that benevolence, even in the face of difficulty.

Each one of us brings to the stories a specific collection of experiences that shapes who we are and how we perceive the world. We respond to the imagery of the story by creating specific images in our mind's eye, images that spring from the well of our individual circumstances, images that evoke strong feelings and have deep personal significance. If we are attentive to these images and let them penetrate our awareness, they can foster a deeper understanding of ourselves as human beings and help us live lives that are richer and more meaningful.

1

A Story Not Told, a Song Not Sung

A Folktale from India Retold

There once was a woman who kept all her songs and all her stories to herself because no one took the time to listen to them. All of her memories and all of her longings remained buried deep within. All of her burdens she carried alone. After a time, her stories and her songs grew restless, for they wanted to be heard. They struggled to come out, but the woman could not share them. Finally, they made their way into her dreams. Night after night, the woman tossed and turned as the stories roiled around inside her. She could not get a decent night's sleep.

"What is the matter with you?" cried her husband.

"I do not know," she replied.

One morning, she was so tired that, after her husband left for work, she lay down on the kitchen floor and fell sound asleep. When she did, her mouth opened wide and she began to snore. The stories and the songs saw their chance to be free. They escaped from the woman's mouth and flew out into the air. They hovered above her, staring down at her sleeping body, all alone on the wooden floor.

"We cannot leave her here," said the stories. "What will she do without us?"

1

The stories turned themselves into a robe and hung on a peg by the bedroom door. The songs became slippers and rested underneath.

When the husband returned from work, he asked his wife, "Who is here?"

"No one," she replied.

"Who belongs to those slippers and that robe?" he demanded.

The wife was at a loss to explain. "I simply do not know," she said.

The husband and the wife began to argue, and when night fell, they still had not settled their dispute. Now, in that village at that time, it was the custom when a couple disagreed and could not settle their quarrel by the end of the day for the husband to spend the night in the Temple of the Monkey King. The husband stormed out of the house and went to the temple. He found a darkened room in the temple, and lay down on the floor to sleep.

The wife sat at the kitchen table and tried to make sense of things. She could not understand what had happened. Finally, she blew out the candle, put her head down on the table, and fell asleep.

Now, in that village when the candle flames were put out at night, they went to the Temple of the Monkey King to chatter and discuss the day's events.

As the husband lay on the floor in the darkened room of the temple, one by one the candle flames danced into the room. They nattered back and forth, waiting for all of the tongues of flame to arrive. After a time, it became clear to the husband that one of the flames was late. "Where is he?" the rest sputtered.

At last, the tardy flame arrived. "Where have you been?" asked the others.

"My couple had an argument," he said. "The husband came home and found a strange robe and slippers by the bedroom door."

"I'm sure he was quite angry!" the others exclaimed.

"Oh yes, but it isn't what he thinks. The woman has stories to tell and songs to sing but no one ever listens. For years, she has kept them all to herself. This morning, while she was sleeping, they found a way out! The stories turned into that robe and the songs became those slippers."

When the husband heard that, he understood what had happened. He got up, walked out of the Temple of the Monkey King, and ran back home. By the light of the moon, he could see his wife slumped over the kitchen table. He awakened her gently. He took the robe and placed it tenderly around her shoulders. He bent down and put the slippers on her feet. Then he sat down at the table and said, "Wife, tell me your stories and sing me your songs. I am here and I will not leave again. Tell me all that you have to say!"

Throughout the night and into the next day, and for many days thereafter, howls of sorrow and peals of laughter filled that kitchen. The woman poured out her stories and her songs while her husband listened, and peace and joy filled both their hearts.

Our lives are shaped by the stories we tell and the stories we cherish. Our greatest spiritual need is to find meaning in our lives. We ask ourselves important questions: Who am I? What does all of this mean? Am I here for a reason? Who are you? How did all of this come to be? As we pause and reflect on our experiences, we try to find the answers to these questions. The events of our lives unfold within a framework of days, weeks, months, and years. We structure this passage of time into beginnings, middles, and ends. The past informs the present and reveals to us our dreams of the future, and we develop perspective. The seemingly random happenings of our days are threaded together and we discover the story of our lives.

If we do not share our stories, we become strangers to ourselves and strangers to one another. Through stories, we establish connections and realize we are not alone. As the other person makes known the details of a life, we recognize bits and pieces of ourselves, and the obstacles that separate us slowly dissolve. We bring to each other the moments of our lives, our fears, our hopes, our joys, and we nourish one another. Our burdens become lighter, our sorrows are eased, and we celebrate the ordinary and extraordinary occurrences in our daily lives.

Baucis and Philemon

A Greek Myth Retold

There are times when the gods become restless with the heavens and grow curious about the earth. They abandon their celestial home and travel the earth where mortals dwell. Long ago, Zeus, father of all the gods and humans, took a notion to leave the lofty peaks of Mount Olympus and visit the people in the land of Phrygia. He asked his son Hermes to join him.

"If we really wish to see how they live, why don't we disguise ourselves as ordinary mortals?" suggested Hermes. Zeus agreed.

Late one afternoon, weary from walking all day, Zeus and Hermes came upon a town nestled in the midst of the hills. They stopped at a house to ask for rest and shelter. But the people in the house refused to let them in. They tried another home and were also denied entry. Door after door they knocked upon, but each and every person in that town turned them away.

"What is the matter with these people?" bellowed Zeus. "Have they forgotten the sacred duty of hospitality? I tell you, this land would be better off without them."

The two shook the dust from their sandals and walked out of the town. In the distance, resting on the side of a hill, they saw a ragged little hut with a thatched roof and a door wide open. A few scraggly chickens wandered in the yard. A small garden was tucked up against the house, and nearby a gnarled apple tree bent toward the ground. "Let us try one more time," said Hermes to his father.

As the two wandered into the yard, an old goose came out from behind the house, squawking and flapping its wings. When he heard the noise, an old man hobbled out of the house. He saw the two men, shooed the goose away, and called out, "My dear sirs, you look tired. Come inside and rest."

The old man led them into the tiny dwelling and called out to his wife, "Baucis, we have guests." The old woman rose from her place by the hearth.

"Welcome, gentlemen," she said as her face broke into a warm smile. "Philemon, pull up a bench so that our guests may sit down." As soon as their guests had settled in, the old couple began to bustle about. Baucis bent over the embers in the hearth, added some wood chips, and fanned them into a blaze. Then she put a pot of water on to boil. Philemon went out into the garden to gather vegetables and herbs.

Zeus and Hermes looked around the humble interior of the one-room cottage. The old couple had little in the way of worldly posses-sions. The furniture was plain and sparse. Earthenware dishes were stacked in the cupboard. Nevertheless, an atmosphere of contentment pervaded the room. Flowers filled a chipped cup sitting on the table. Herbs hung from the rafters. A basket of fresh eggs rested in the corner.

Philemon returned with a huge cabbage, a handful of onions, and some radishes. As the old couple prepared the meal, they worked side by side in a rhythm forged from many years of living together. They chattered to each other and entertained their guests with stories of their days and the history of the place. They had lived together for many long years, and times had often been quite hard, but their love and companionship had helped them shoulder their burdens.

The presence of visitors seemed to bring an air of festivity to the place, and Baucis and Philemon responded with warmth and gen-erosity. Philemon pulled a bench toward the table and put sedge-filled cushions on it so that the two men would be more comfortable.

Baucis covered the cushions with a coarsely woven linen cloth, one that she saved for special occasions. As she rubbed down the table with a handful of fresh mint, she noticed, as if for the first time, that one of the table legs was shorter than the rest. So Baucis took a piece of old tile and tucked it underneath to level the table. She held a bowl of warmed water before her guests so that they could wash their hands. Philemon placed the earthenware dishes and beechwood cups on the table. He took an earthenware pitcher and filled it with wine, not aged but new, and placed it in the center of the table.

Then the meal was served, a repast of simple and hearty fare, but more food than Baucis and Philemon ate in a week. They started with eggs baked lightly in the ash, radishes, olives, cherries pickled in wine, endive. A rich cabbage and onion soup was the main course. Afterward, there were apples, plums, and a thick piece of honeycomb to sweeten any of the fruit if it was sour. But as the meal wore on, the old couple began to notice something peculiar happening. Philemon had poured all of the wine he had into the earthenware pitcher. However, each time the last cup of wine was served, the pitcher seemed to miraculously refill itself. Baucis and Philemon became uneasy.

Finally, Philemon bowed his head and in a faltering voice said, "Sirs, my wife and I took you to be simple folk, like ourselves. But now, I wonder …" He hesitated before continuing, "Who are you …?"

Zeus spoke gently. "You are right. We are not ordinary mortals. We are gods come down from Mount Olympus."

Philemon gasped. "Please, my dear sirs, I apologize for our plain fare. If you are not satisfied, I'm sure we can find something more suitable." He glanced about the room and his eyes fell on the old goose who had wandered inside. "Our goose might make a fine meal, if we stewed her long enough."

Hermes reached out and stroked its long neck. "Do not harm your old goose," he said tenderly. "Your food was just what we needed."

Zeus spoke once more. "The people in this land have grown selfish and heartless. They will be punished. Only the two of you have shown us kindness. Save yourselves and come with us now!"

Baucis and Philemon stood up. They reached for their walking sticks and followed the gods out the door. Zeus and Hermes climbed up the hillside as the old couple trailed slowly behind. When they reached the top, Zeus turned and glared at the valley below. Baucis and Philemon followed his stony stare and gasped at what they saw. The valley was engulfed in water, all trace of houses, roads, and people obliterated. The floodwaters raged upward, stopping just before they reached the old couple's home.

Baucis and Philemon could not take their eyes away from the scene below. Ever so slowly, the waters receded and, as they did, the little hut began to change. The straw on the roof became denser and brighter until they saw that it was made of gold. The wooden posts holding up the roof turned to marble. And the door became silver, intricately patterned and worked.

Zeus gazed affectionately at the husband and wife. "My dear Baucis and Philemon, you have opened your home and your hearts to Hermes and myself. What can I offer you in return?"

Philemon was slow to respond. He bent his head toward Baucis and the two of them spoke together quietly. He nodded and then turned to Zeus. "All we ask is to be able to stay in the place that is familiar to us. Let us serve you in the temple that you have created," and he pointed to their transformed dwelling. "Oh, and one more thing," said Philemon slowly. "We have been together for so long that we cannot bear the thought of being apart, not even for a moment. Please let us die at the same time."

Touched by their unassuming nature and love for each other, Zeus honored Baucis and Philemon's request. For many years after the flood, they continued to live and serve in that place. But one day, as they stood together next to the temple, they felt a change come over them. Their feet sank into the earth and began to take root. Baucis looked at her husband. His arms stretched into branches and leaves began to sprout from his fingertips.

"Good-bye, my dearest love," she whispered. Philemon leaned toward his wife.

"Farewell, my love."

Their weathered old skin turned to bark and they were gone. In their place stood a linden tree and an oak tree, forever entwined.

In the Hebrew Bible, three strangers appear to Abraham as he sits outside his tent under the oak of Mamre. He and his wife, Sarah, welcome the men into their tent, graciously offering them repose and sustenance in fulfillment of an ancient code of hospitality. The strangers extend Yahweh's promise to the couple and announce that Sarah, an old woman, will have a child within a year. There are many works of art based on this passage from Genesis, including the famous icon Philoxenia of Abraham, *painted by Andrei Rublev, which uses this scene to represent the Christian Holy Trinity.*

Philoxenia comes from the Greek and means "love of strangers." This ideal of hospitality goes beyond the mere implementation of an obligatory code of etiquette. Foreigners in ancient Greece did not enjoy the rights of citizenship. However, the Greeks developed an ethic of welcoming strangers by placing them under the protection of the god Zeus. When you received a stranger into a public sanctuary or your home, it became a sacred act.

Cultivating an attitude of hospitality can mean several things. We can embrace the stranger, the one who is often rejected or marginalized, and treat that person with respect and kindness, opening up a space in our day-to-day lives where the stranger can feel welcome and valued. It can also mean developing a stance of openness toward the many possibilities that life offers to us. Our fears, our difficulties, even our creative urges and dreams often seem strange to us and we turn away from them. However, if we accept and welcome these things, they can provide us with opportunities for change and growth.

Catch-the-Wind

A Slavic Folktale Retold

There was once a town, tucked down in the palm of a valley, filled with forthright people who earnestly followed the book of rules. Once a month, a traveling magistrate visited the town to administer justice and settle disputes. The mayor kept a record of all grievances in his absence. On the day of the magistrate's arrival, those with complaints hurried to the town hall. The mayor consulted his list and patiently lined up the plaintiffs. One by one, he called them up to the judge's bench to plead their case. The magistrate was a busy man who was only interested in hearing the facts. As he listened to each problem, he rested his chin on his hand as if the weight of personal detail were too much for him to bear. "Enough," he announced gruffly when he had collected the necessary information. Then he opened the pages of a well-worn book and issued a decision based on a complex system of laws. At times, the magistrate's penalties seemed too harsh; at other times, they felt too lenient. Nevertheless, the people believed this was the best way to maintain order and unity. They accepted the judge's decrees and tried to live with each other as best they could.

One day, the magistrate arrived as usual. People filed into the town hall to await justice. Instead of seating himself, the magistrate stood in front of the bench and announced, "The king has declared that this town is too small to warrant my services. From now on, you must settle your disputes among yourselves!" He clutched the law book under his arm. The people watched in dismay as the magistrate and his rules disappeared from view.

That evening, the mayor called together the wisest men in the village. They assembled around the potbellied stove, their grave faces lined with worry. The mayor initiated the discussion. "What shall we do?" he asked.

One by one, the men stated their concerns. "What will happen to us?"

"No one here is qualified to decide what is right and wrong."

"Who will be the voice of justice?" The men began to argue back and forth.

The mayor's housekeeper, a woman who had seen many years, entered the room carrying a coal scuttle. As she tended the fire, she listened to their deliberations, shaking her head or clicking her tongue after each man spoke. Finally, with an exasperated sigh, she turned to the men and said, "Excuse me, sirs, may I say something?"

The mayor's eyes circled the room with a questioning gaze. The men nodded their heads in agreement. The old woman straightened herself and began, "The rules are not written in books. They are written in your hearts. People know what is right and what is wrong. If they listen to one another, they will know what to do."

The men sat in silence. As they mulled over the housekeeper's words, their faces crumpled with doubt. "But who will be the judge?" asked the mayor skeptically.

The old woman settled herself in an empty chair next to the stove and smiled. "Let me tell you a story," she said.

"Once, there was a village rooted in rugged, green hills that reached into the sea like stony fingers. Their rocky banks sheltered a busy harbor with ships that sailed to and from nearby ports. The people of this town were fair-minded and wished to live together peacefully. In the center of the town, they constructed a simple tower made of four sturdy timbers, topped by a red-tiled roof. Inside the tower they hung a large bell with a rope that dangled onto the ground. Around the bell tower they placed a row of solid wooden benches. 'Any one of us who feels wronged can come and ring this bell,' the people declared. 'When the bell rings, we will gather on these benches, listen to the person's story, and settle the dispute.'

"At first the bell rang often. When the townsfolk heard the chimes peal, they would set aside their tasks, hasten to the square, and sit together on the benches. The aggrieved person stood underneath the bell and unfolded the details of the situation. As the people listened, unhurried, to the story, they were able to understand the problem and resolve the grievance. As time wore on, a change came over that town and the bell rang less and less often. Merchants treated their customers with respect. Neighbors looked after one another. Husbands were gentler with their wives. The villagers cared for each other with tenderness and compassion.

"Outside of the village, perched on a hill that rose high above everything else, stood the magnificent house of the wealthy merchant Domazhir. At the front of the house, two ornately carved wooden doors opened out onto a wide porch made of thick oak planks. Tall cedar pillars stretched from the porch like ancient trees to support the great tiled roof that capped the house. Domazhir could hear the faint peals of the bell from that porch. He knew what the pealing of the bell meant and accepted its necessity, but he never joined the villagers. He preferred to stand on his porch and peer down into the town to observe the comings and goings of the people below.

"Domazhir surrounded himself with valuable things. His house was filled with fine brocades, gold and silver plates, exquisite works of art. Domazhir was very proud of all these possessions, but nothing gave him more pleasure than his stable of horses. His stable was almost as grand as his house and contained the finest horses in the land. Each animal was a flawless specimen of a particular breed. All the stalls, save one, were filled. Domazhir was still searching for the perfect horse to occupy the empty space.

"One morning, a huge three-masted ship with blood-red sails slipped through the mist and entered the harbor. A majestic stallion emerged from beneath the deck. The animal was restless after being confined and began to stomp his hooves and tug on the reins that were held tightly in his trainer's hands. The horse reared up on its hind legs and uttered a shrill whinny that pierced the damp air. The people on the wharf turned toward the sound. Through the fog, they saw a horse quite unlike any they had ever seen before. It was dapple-gray with a jet-black mane and a tail that curled like ocean waves. It stood so tall that its obsidian hooves seemed to scrape the sky.

"The trainer enlisted the help of a nearby sailor. The sailor grabbed hold of the bridle while the trainer gripped the reins. With great difficulty, the two men led the uneasy horse onto the dock and up the path toward the village. When the horse sensed the openness of the market square, it lurched forward and broke free from the men's grasp. The gray stallion charged through the village and galloped up the path that led to Domazhir's house.

"When the stallion broke free, Domazhir watched from the edge of his veranda. The horse raced up the path, its reins flapping in the air. Domazhir could see the strength ripple through its muscles as its mighty hooves hammered against the earth. His keen gaze followed the horse as it rounded the bend and climbed the rocky incline toward his house. It showed no signs of stopping. Domazhir took a deep breath and opened his doors wide. The horse bounded up the porch steps and bolted into the house.

"In a whirlwind of fury, the stallion thrashed and kicked, smashing tables and splintering chairs. Domazhir crept across the threshold and inched his way toward the horse. The horse snorted and stomped its foot. Domazhir held his breath and did not move. When the stallion finally raised its head toward Domazhir, the man tentatively stretched out his hand and gently stroked the horse's velvety muzzle. Domazhir leaned over, caught the reins, and vaulted onto the horse's back. He urged the stallion through the open doors and the horse leapt off the porch. Together they rode out onto the ridge that overlooked the sea. Domazhir felt the echo of the surf in the hoofbeats of the horse as it thundered across the ground. They left the path and rode into the wild hills. The horse never tired. Time disappeared for Domazhir. He felt as if nothing in the world could harm him.

"As the day began to lose its light, horse and rider cantered into the stable yard. Domazhir did not call for the stable master to attend to his horse, as was his usual custom. Instead, he slipped from the horse's back, gently clasped its bridle, and led the stallion into the stall closest to the house, the one that had remained empty for so long. He took the currycomb and as he brushed away the dirt and dust, he could feel the beat of the horse's heart, hear the rhythm of its breath. 'You run as if you thought you could catch the wind,' he whispered. 'That is what I shall call you: Catch-the-Wind.'

"After that, Catch-the-Wind was the only horse Domazhir would ride. He never put a saddle on the horse, never allowed anyone else to groom or ride him. When Catch-the-Wind heard Domazhir's footsteps in the yard, his ears pricked up. He leaned his head over the stall gate and greeted his master with a soft whinny. Every day the two would ride out into the untamed places. Fishermen watched as they galloped along the gravel beach where the surf crashed into the craggy cliffs. The villagers looked up and saw horse and rider silhouetted against the pale gray sky as they rode along the ridge. Soon everyone in that town knew that the dapple-gray horse who had run away from the red-sailed ship had found a home in Domazhir's stable.

"One evening, Domazhir and Catch-the-Wind were returning home after a long business trip. Wind-swept clouds sailed across the moon's full face. Domazhir decided to take a shortcut through the forest because they had been riding for most of the day. Moonlight edged through the tangle of trees as Domazhir guided Catch-the-Wind along the path where shadows flickered wildly. Suddenly, six robbers carrying spears and knives jumped out from behind the trees. Three were on horseback and three were on foot. Two of the men rushed forward and tried to grab Catch-the-Wind by the bridle. When Catch-the-Wind felt a stranger's hand on his bridle, he reared up, slashing the air with his huge hooves as Domazhir held tight to the reins. His hooves smashed into the thieves and knocked them to the ground. Another bandit ran toward the horse with his spear raised. Catch–the–Wind rushed right at him and toppled the outlaw with his huge, broad chest. Aware that the trees held danger, the stallion dashed forward and began to race through the forest. The mounted thieves pursued Domazhir and his horse, but they were no match for Catch–the–Wind.

"Sweating and out of breath, Catch–the–Wind reached the safety of the stable yard. Domazhir quickly dismounted, but when he did, he saw that his faithful steed had been wounded. A horrible gash lay across the animal's left flank. Blood poured out of the cut, streaming down its leg and matting the horse's tail. Domazhir bellowed out for the stable master to come quickly. When he arrived, Domazhir wailed, 'Look at my horse. You must do something!' Domazhir stood off to one side as the stable master tenderly washed and dressed the horse's wound. He recounted the terrifying details of the evening's events.

"'You owe your life to this horse!' replied the stable master. Domazhir stretched out on the straw in Catch–the–Wind's stall to sleep but he could not close his eyes, for the night was punctuated by the pain-filled whinnies of his wounded steed. In the pale morning light, Domazhir arose. He stared at his horse's marred flank and shuddered.

"Catch–the–Wind's wound took a long time to heal. Domazhir visited his horse daily but he did not linger long. The ragged slash in the horse's flesh glared out at him, and he could not bring himself to run his hand over the horse's blemished body. He relegated the task of grooming Catch–the–Wind to a stable boy. Without the passion of those wild rides, his days dulled into a gray routine and he began to grow restless. 'When will Catch–the–Wind be ready to ride?' he inquired of the stable master, his voiced edged with impatience.

"Finally, Catch–the–Wind seemed strong enough to be ridden. Domazhir gingerly mounted his stallion, carefully avoiding the jagged red scar that had replaced the gaping wound. As Catch–the–Wind galloped out onto the familiar ridge, his master felt the wind's caress on his face. A delighted smile lit up his face as he closed his eyes and breathed in the fresh salt air. The stallion sprinted across the ridge eagerly with his head held high, but after a few miles, it was obvious to Domazhir that his horse did not run with the same vigor and vitality as before. Catch-the-Wind grew tired and slowed his pace. Domazhir urged the horse on, but Catch-the-Wind began to breathe heavily and they were forced to return to the stable. Domazhir was determined to regain the pleasure of those unruly excursions before Catch-the-Wind was injured. Day after day, he took Catch-the-Wind out for short rides, hoping to build up the horse's strength, but the stallion's stamina did not return.

"The horse's diminished might deprived Domazhir of more fearless rides into the wilderness. It was as if the slash to Catch-the-Wind's flesh had allowed vulnerability to seep into Domazhir's life. Catch-the-Wind became a painful reminder of what Domazhir had lost. He came to the horse's stall less and less often, until finally he no longer visited Catch-the-Wind. With no one to ride him, the animal was turned out to pasture. Catch-the-Wind remained eager to run. The stallion's pent-up energy surged beyond the limits of the fence. One day he came upon some downed fenceposts, leaped over them, and escaped into the wild hills.

"At first, Catch-the-Wind was able to find shelter and food in those hills. However, an unusually harsh winter set in. He browsed the tips of pine trees and pawed the frozen earth looking for hidden roots, but there was little food to eat. The outline of his ribs became visible through his ragged coat. The trees and rocks offered scant shelter from the bitter wind, and the horse's bony frame shivered with the cold. In desperation, Catch-the-Wind made his way out of the hills into the town, looking for food and warmth. He wandered into the center of the village and began to scrape the rocky soil underneath the bell tower, searching for roots to eat. His hoof struck the bell rope and a single distinct note pierced the night. As Catch-the-Wind continued to strike the ground, the bell rang out loud and clear. When the villagers heard the bell, they put on their coats and shawls, grabbed lanterns, and made their way to the town square. The night was chilly and damp; flakes of frost hung in the air. The villagers held their lamps high and in the glittering darkness tried to make out the strange figure under the bell tower. 'Who is there?' they called out, but received only a soft snort in reply.

"'Why, it's a horse ringing the bell,' someone said, and they began to chuckle.

"'It's not just any horse,' said a young man. 'It's Catch-the-Wind.'

"'No,' said a village merchant, 'this can't be Catch-the-Wind. Look at his dull coat, his tangled mane. Why, his ribs are showing.'

"'Ahh, look again,' said an old woman. 'No other horse has a dappled gray coat with a black mane and tail.' As the townspeople moved closer, the horse remained strangely quiet.

"'But how can such a thing be possible? He is the favorite horse of Domazhir,' said someone else.

"'I work in Domazhir's stable,' said the young man who had identified Catch-the-Wind. He took an apple out of his coat pocket and offered it to the horse. As Catch-the-Wind chomped noisily on the apple, the stable hand grasped his bridle and related the story. 'One night Master Domazhir and Catch-the-Wind were riding through the forest when they were attacked by a band of thieves. Catch-the-Wind trampled the bandits and fled to safety. He saved Domazhir's life, but received a cut to his flank from which he never fully recovered. He was never the same again and could not run as before. Domazhir ignored him and turned him out to pasture. When the horse ran away, the Master never even went to look for him. He seemed relieved that the horse had disappeared from sight.'

"Despite the cold, the townspeople sat on the benches and listened. 'Let us fetch Domazhir,' they said. Two of the strongest men were chosen. They climbed the rocky path that led to Domazhir's mansion and pounded on the huge wooden doors.

"Surprisingly, Domazhir himself answered the door. He looked questioningly at the two men. 'The bell has rung. You have been summoned to the town square,' said the two men emphatically.

"Domazhir's eyes narrowed slightly, but he understood that it was his duty to go. As he donned his fur coat, he asked the men, 'Can you tell me what this is about?'

"'It's about one of your horses,' they replied. Domazhir walked silently through the chilly night as he followed the men into the village and up to the bell tower.

"At the sound of Domazhir's footsteps, Catch-the-Wind's ears flicked and the horse raised its head. The assembled crowd turned toward Domazhir. An old woman stood up and, facing Domazhir, spoke. 'Look at your horse, Domazhir! Look at Catch-the-Wind!' Domazhir did not move as he peered at the faded form of his once mighty stallion. He saw the scar, the rail-thin body, the matted mane and tail. He also saw the stable boy's hands, one clutching the bridle, the other caressing the muzzle of the horse. He remembered a time when only he could clasp that bridle, when Catch-the-Wind bristled at a stranger's touch. The villagers gathered around the horse and master. The old woman continued. 'This is your horse, a horse that remained faithful to you and saved your life. In return, you ignored it. You must take Catch-the-Wind back to your stable. Domazhir, you must promise to take care of your horse. You, Domazhir, not your stable boy, not the stable master, must care for this horse.'

"Domazhir nodded his head, 'I will do as you say. I promise.' He grabbed the old leather bridle and gently led the animal through the crowd. He slowly trudged up the hill, carefully guiding the gaunt stallion, and he recalled that night, so long ago, when Catch-the-Wind had fought off the bandits. The long-hidden memory of his panic surfaced, and he remembered how he shook with fear as Catch-the-Wind courageously rode through the darkness.

"Domazhir brought Catch-the-Wind into his old stall and wrapped the horse in a blanket. He called for the stable master. 'Show me how to make a warm mash. My horse is starving.' He listened closely to the instructions, mixed the food, and held the bucket for the hungry horse. That night Domazhir slept in the stall with his horse. The next day, he spent hours brushing Catch-the-Wind's dull coat and combing the burrs and snarls from his tangled mane and tail.

"Domazhir worked side by side with the stable master and learned how to care for his horse. He rubbed liniment into Catch-the-Wind's aching joints, cleaned the animal's damaged hooves, and spoon-fed him a special tonic that he made himself. Each and every day, he came to the stable and tended to Catch-the-Wind's needs. Working in the stable gave Domazhir a great deal of satisfaction, and he was proud of his newly developed skills and abilities. Domazhir found that he looked forward to spending time with Catch-the-Wind, and he rummaged through the kitchen to find special treats for the animal, bringing him carrots, apples, and lumps of brown sugar. Slowly, under Domazhir's tender care, Catch-the-Wind's strength returned.

"The snows of winter melted and green grass poked through the brown earth. Catch-the-Wind sniffed the spring air and fidgeted in his stall. Pleased that his horse's energy and spirit had returned, Domazhir took Catch-the-Wind to the pasture and turned him loose. As Catch-the-Wind frisked about, Domazhir leaned over the fence and laughed with delight. One warm afternoon, Domazhir decided to take the horse for a ride. He climbed onto the stallion's back and the two trotted out onto the ridge. A soft breeze tousled Domazhir's hair as Catch-the-Wind gradually picked up speed and galloped along the path. The familiar sense of power returned to Domazhir, but now this feeling was tinged with a deeper understanding of what had been gained and what had been lost. When Catch-the-Wind inevitably grew tired, Domazhir slipped off the stallion's back without regret. He saw the ragged scar on the horse's flank and didn't cringe. The blemish was no longer a painful reminder of loss. Instead, it was a sign of endurance and a testament to what he and his horse had earned through perseverance. Domazhir reached out his hand and gently stroked the scar. Then he reached up, tenderly clasped Catch-the-Wind's bridle, and walked his horse back to the stable."

The housekeeper's story had taken all night to unfold. When she finished, the men let the story settle in their hearts and then, slowly, with great deliberateness, they began to speak. The mayor started the conversation: "Let us gather in the town hall."

"Not to complain," said the man next to him, "but to listen to each other's concerns." "Yes," said another man, "let us make a circle of understanding." And that is exactly what the people did.

Patient listening can provide an opportunity for healing to begin. We affirm people and offer a safe place for them to reveal their deepest worries and longings. It takes time to listen well, to permit the many false starts and extraneous details to spill out before the essence of the matter bubbles to the surface. When we truly listen to each other, we hollow out a space within us where we can shelter another person's story.

Listening involves attentiveness, selflessness, and empathy. We must set aside our perceptions and our judgments to allow other people to explain who they are and how they think. Not only do we hear the words spoken, we try to plumb the depths of what is beneath the words, listening for the unspoken fears, hopes, hurts, and insecurities that are often verbalized as complaints, boasts, or excuses. We accept the story as a gift, a thing to be treasured, not a problem to be solved or an idea requiring an opinion. In this way, we faithfully carry the stories of others with us and are mindful of the grace of their presence in our lives.

4

Because I Can

A Tale from the Middle East Retold

The marketplace buzzed with the hustle and bustle of commerce. Need rubbed up against desire as merchants haggled with customers while beggars droned their pleas and pickpockets threaded their way unobtrusively through the swarm of shoppers. The footsteps of the crowd churned the dust upward to accompany the swirl of agitated voices.

Shaded by an awning at the edge of the square, a group of five men sipped coffee and discussed the affairs of the day. They piled opinions on top of self-assurance, reinforcing their view of the world and confirming their place in it. As they chatted on, a gaunt woman approached from the bazaar. Her pleading words penetrated the conversation. "Gentlemen, can one of you spare a coin or two so that a poor woman can feed her family?"

When she stretched forth her empty hand, the men abruptly stopped talking. She extended her upturned palm toward each man in turn, inviting a response. One by one their faces slackened from rigid composure into discomfiture as each man measured her need against his own obligation.

The last man in the circle was well known for his generosity and kindness. As soon as he heard the woman's entreaty, he reached into his pocket. When she turned to him, he pulled out a handful of coins, poured them into her palm until it was full, then motioned for her to put out her other hand and gave her the remaining coins. Tears slid down the woman's face as she bowed low in gratitude. "May Allah bless you, kind sir. Now, I can feed all of my children. You have saved us!"

After she departed, the other men voiced their irritation. "What did you do that for?" said one.

"It was not necessary," commented another. "After all, you gave your *zakat* (required contribution) yesterday. You were not obliged to give her anything."

"Be careful. The next thing you know, every beggar in the marketplace will be after you!" warned a third.

"She would have been happy with a couple of coins," said a fourth. "You certainly didn't have to give her so much."

The generous man answered their objections. "I have so much and she asked for so little. She may not know what I possess, but I do. I could not be satisfied with myself if I did not give her what I am able to share."

The third pillar, or requirement, of Islam is called zakat. *It is compulsory for every Muslim who possesses sufficient means to pay a portion to the poor. It is the right of the needy to receive this tax and they are not indebted to those who pay it. In this way, a relationship between the affluent and the destitute is made possible, and the distribution of wealth ensures that the poor are not abandoned.*

A spirit of generosity enlarges our view of the world. We move beyond our narrow, selfish concerns and our desire to accumulate material goods to recognize the needs of others. As our perspective shifts, the hardships faced by other people often force us to appreciate our own good fortune. By acknowledging the blessings that we have received, we gain an understanding of what is important to us and are grateful. Our thankfulness encourages us to share our money, time, and talents to help alleviate the burdens of those around us. In this way, we honor the gifts we have been given.

5

The Juggler and the Priest
A French Miracle Tale Retold

gentle autumn breeze whispered through the branches of an old poplar tree and loosened a trembling shower of golden leaves that fluttered onto the cobbled stones beneath it. An itinerant juggler stood at the edge of the market square. He saw the tree but was unmoved by its resplendent beauty. His trained eye surveyed the village terrain. Two narrow streets lined with shops and apartments converged in the center of the market square. A low, stone wall with a rusty iron gate in the middle curved around the other side. The poplar tree rose up next to the open gate. It provided the perfect setting for his performance.

The juggler tugged on the halter of his donkey and ambled toward the tree. As he tethered the animal to the gatepost, he glimpsed the well-worn path that led from the gate to a tiny stone church beyond. He noted the church, the shabby rectory behind it, and the tilting headstones of the cemetery, then quickly turned away. While the juggler untied his pack, he observed the townsfolk. A few shopkeepers stood beside their storefronts, the dullness of the afternoon resting idly on their shoulders. Several mothers and their children strolled along the sunlit streets. A dog barked in the distance.

"Just ripe for a little entertainment," thought the juggler to himself. With practiced flair, he began to take out the contents of his pack, pretending not to notice the townsfolk. He put on his patterned tunic, his slippers with bells on the toes, his brightly colored cap. As expected, the villagers grew curious.

A merchant from across the street called out, "Ahhhh, a street musician, a *jongleur*! Let us see what he has to offer." The juggler pulled from his bag a small hoop decorated with ribbons and waved it with a flourish. He drew purple and red scarves out of his rucksack and beckoned to the children. When a suitable number of people had assembled, the juggler carefully set out a wooden bowl for contributions. He picked up his flute, brought it to his lips, and began his routine. Effortlessly, he executed a skillful series of tricks, calculated to excite the crowd. The familiar exclamations of the onlookers echoed in his ears as he spun plates on sticks, balanced a stack of objects on his nose, and juggled scarves, hoops, and pins.

Finally, the juggler brandished several balls of different colors in his hands. "Ladies and gentlemen, I have saved the best for last. I will spin for you ... a rainbow!" The spectators mumbled their approval. The juggler lifted his hand to toss the first ball and, at that moment, the church bell rang out. The group shifted its gaze toward the churchyard.

"Come, it's time for Mass," announced a young mother as she reached down to grab her little boy's hand. She nodded her thanks to the juggler, dropped a coin in the bowl, and walked through the gate. Several others did the same. As the bell continued to chime, people came out of the apartments and made their way to church.

A solitary merchant remained in front of the juggler. He looked around, shook his head, and chuckled. "It was a good show," he remarked. "Too bad it had to end so soon!" He flipped two coins into the bowl. The juggler smiled his thanks and leaned over. He counted the coins in the bottom of the bowl. There was just enough to pay for a night's lodging.

Footsteps clattered on the cobblestones and the juggler looked up to see a woman hurrying across the market square. Years of worry had traced deep lines onto her face and her disheveled hair was more gray than brown. Her fingers clutched a threadbare red shawl around shoulders bent with fatigue. She paid no attention to the juggler as she rushed by. At the iron gate, the woman paused and released her weariness with a deep sigh. Her fists relaxed their hold on her shawl. With worn hands, she tidied her hair, shook the dust from her skirt, and walked down the path.

The remnants of the juggler's act lay scattered on the ground. Slowly, he gathered up his things and returned them to his well-worn rucksack. The warm autumn breeze carried the reverent murmurs of the villagers through the open church doors and floated them into the market square. The holy hum of their voices reached the ears of the juggler and flowed into an empty space in his heart. He lifted his pack onto the donkey's back and reached out to untie the animal. To his own surprise, the juggler let go of the rope, left his donkey tied, and walked into the church.

The juggler slipped silently into a pew in the rear of the tiny church and allowed his eyes to adjust to the sheltering dimness of the candlelit sanctuary. The townsfolk knelt solemnly, staring straight ahead. He followed their gaze to the front of the church where an old priest stood before the stone altar performing the ancient ritual of the mass. They responded to his intonations with familiar recitations, becoming one voice united in prayer. When the priest elevated the golden chalice in his hands, the congregation raised their eyes heavenward and allowed silence to suffuse the chapel. At the end of the mass, the priest faced the people and, smiling tenderly, blessed them. Chatting softly to one another, the villagers filed out of the church.

Outside, their laughter and gossip became robust. The juggler remained inside. The stillness of the church surrounded him and he was reluctant to leave. To the right of the altar he saw a wooden statue of the Virgin balancing the Christ Child in her arms. Standing before the statue was the haggard woman he had seen rushing across the square. She whispered a conversation to the impassive figure, as if Our Lady could hear and respond to her pleas. With great tenderness, she stretched out her knobby fingers and stroked the frozen hem of the Virgin's robe. When she turned around, the juggler noticed that her look of worry had softened and her face now radiated a serene calm.

The parishioners drifted out of the churchyard and returned, refreshed, to the customary rhythm of their day. The old priest stepped quietly into the church. Seeing the juggler sitting in the shadows, he walked toward him and greeted him. "You have the look of a traveling man," he remarked with a welcoming smile. "What brings you to this tiny parish?"

The juggler turned his head and answered flatly, "The townsfolk seemed in need of a diversion. I indulged their interest!"

"Ah, you are a performer. It is a worthy thing to do. It helps lighten the load. People carry big burdens; they need to be lifted out of themselves," said the priest as he took a seat next to the juggler.

"I suppose so," said the juggler. "Sometimes I think I just help them pass the time."

"Sometimes, that is just what is needed."

"Maybe ..." The juggler's voice trailed off.

"You must see many interesting things in your travels. Meet many different kinds of people. Is it very exciting?" inquired the priest.

"Not as exciting as you might think," said the juggler with a wry smile. "After a while, one town seems much like the next."

"It must be lonely at times as well ... terribly lonely," said the priest. The tenderness in the old man's words peeled away the layer of hardness the juggler used as a shield and exposed the emptiness that had seeped into his heart. The juggler leaned back against the pew, allowed his shoulders to droop and released a weary sigh.

"You are too young to be so worn out. You need a rest. Come ... stay here for a while."

The juggler could not find words to give shape to the feelings trickling forth. "Why ... what would I do here?" he murmured hesitantly.

"I have a garden in need of harvesting and a rectory and church that require a few simple repairs. You'll have a place to sleep and enough to eat."

The juggler searched the old man's face and when he had convinced himself that the offer was genuine, he nodded his acceptance. "Thank you," he whispered. The juggler collected his things, stabled his donkey in the priest's cowshed, and quietly let go of his wandering life.

After an early breakfast, the priest ushered the juggler into his enormous garden behind the rectory. Gazing out at the rows of vegetables and the bountiful crop of herbs, the juggler declared his confusion. "Seems like a lot of food for one man."

"Hardly enough," said the old man in reply. "You'll see."

The priest showed the juggler how to harvest the earth's generous offerings. He explained the knack of gently removing a potato plant from the ground, shaking the tiny potatoes from the delicate roots, and carefully hoeing out the larger ones from the soil. He demonstrated how to pull up turnips and cut cabbages from their stalks. When they came to the herbs, the old man's voice became tinged with affection. He bent down and tenderly plucked a bright green leaf from a basil plant and held it to the juggler's nose. "Smell that," he invited the young man. "Vegetables are uncomplicated," he said, "but herbs have an amazing complexity. Their intricacies cannot be discovered in a day." For the remainder of the morning, the juggler carefully coaxed potato plants out of the soil and heaped potatoes into tidy piles. In the afternoon, he cut thyme, sage, and winter savory. As he tied the herbs into neat bundles, he inhaled their heady scent and slowly began to distinguish one fragrance from another. The juggler stayed in the garden until the pale autumn sunlight threw long shadows across the soil.

After years fraught with managing the unpredictability of spectators, the juggler found the straightforwardness of his garden responsibilities soothing. His days took on a structure that he could measure in piles of potatoes and in the number of cabbages and turnips stacked in the vegetable bins. His old habit of marching over the terrain, intent only on mapping a route and reaching a destination, softened as the gentle touch of the elements awakened his dormant senses. He felt the warmth of the sun caress his bent back as he worked in the rich, dark soil and breathed in the fragrant earth. One afternoon, time melted into wonder as he watched a rust-and-saffron-patterned butterfly dance across a vibrant patch of zinnias.

On the morning of his third day, as he was hauling potatoes to the shed in a wheelbarrow, the juggler heard a hesitant knocking. He turned to see a nervous young woman at the back door of the rectory. She held a limp burlap sack at her side. On the other side, a skinny little boy stood clinging to the edge of her apron. The old priest opened the door and greeted her with a reassuring smile. They chatted briefly in the open doorway and then walked briskly out into the garden. The woman stood patiently in the middle of the garden, holding open her sack, as the priest put in a generous supply of potatoes, a cabbage, and two medium-sized turnips. Her little boy peeked out shyly from behind the folds of her skirt. The old man tied the bag with twine and hoisted it into her open arms. She thanked him, gave an embarrassed nod to the juggler, and, with her little boy trailing behind, hurried away. The priest called out to the juggler, "You are doing fine work, fine work ..." and returned to the rectory. Later that afternoon, the old man once again entered the garden carrying a basket in his arms. He filled it with vegetables and then, taking out his pocketknife, began to cut zinnias until he had assembled a brightly colored bouquet. He waved good-bye to the juggler and made his way past the rectory, through the churchyard, and out into the street.

That evening, as the juggler and the priest sat down to eat their simple meal of soup and bread, the juggler slyly remarked, "You are making my work easier. If you keep giving things away, I will have less to move into the shed."

The old priest laughed. "Well, you are here to rest. I don't want you to work too hard." He broke off a piece of bread and dipped it into his bowl of soup. The smile on his face crumpled. "There are many in this parish in need. The woman who came here with her little boy has a husband who would rather spend his time in taverns than in the fields. She has four little ones and struggles to keep food on the table. I planted an extra row of potatoes just for her. This afternoon I took some necessities to the old man who lives over the butcher shop. His wife died last spring. They had been married for over fifty years and it takes all of his energy to battle the loneliness. The butcher and I make sure he has enough food and we try to keep him company."

The juggler continued to harvest the garden's bounty and store it safely. The weakened sunlight no longer warmed the days, and the juggler began to spend his time indoors, doing odd jobs in the rectory and the church. The rectory bore the jumbled trappings of daily life; a kitchen table littered with vegetables awaiting a cook's hand, cobwebs overlooked in dusty corners, a cat curled up in a chair with well-worn upholstery. The vaulted interior of the church exhibited an air of unruffled permanence. The two tidy rows of simple oak pews sat stolidly facing the stone altar. On the wall behind the altar, the crucifix looked out over the entire church. Standing on a pedestal in a corner was the hazelwood statue of the Virgin holding the Christ Child. Next to the statue was the only messy thing in the entire church, an iron rack that held three rows of votive candles, which were all different heights and dripped puddles of melted wax over the rim of the rack and onto the floor below. The parishioners lighted the candles as a reminder to Mary and her Child that the frayed edges of their lives needed repair.

Once a week, the juggler scraped the wax from the iron rack and replaced the spent stubs with fresh, unlit candles. One morning, the juggler stepped into the sacristy to fetch a fresh supply of candles. As he came out of the doorway, he saw a young woman standing before the statue. Her tear-stained face looked up at the Virgin and her hands were stretched outward in supplication. The juggler stopped and waited silently. The young woman carried on a whispered conversation with the silent figure of Mary, as if the motionless statue could hear and answer her call. Then she kissed her own fingertip, tenderly stroked the Virgin's wooden robe, turned, and left the church. When the juggler set down his candles by the iron rack, he noticed a tiny knitted sock tucked at the foot of the statue. He ran after the young woman, calling out, "Wait, I think you forgot something," holding up the little sock between his thumb and forefinger. She turned and the juggler saw the anguish in her face.

"No," she answered softly, "I left it for Our Lady. I want her to remember my baby, my poor little boy who is no longer with me. I want her to keep an eye on him in heaven." The juggler felt a pang of sympathy for the young mother.

"I'm so sorry. I'll put it back where I found it," he replied. He returned the sock to the pedestal. Next to the statue's solid wooden foot, the limp, little sock seemed lonely and deserted. The juggler looked up at the statue and found himself hoping that the straight-faced Virgin responded to petitions. "Take care of that little boy," he allowed himself to murmur aloud.

The old priest had a flair for cooking and readily combined herbs, meat, and vegetables into appetizing combinations that filled the kitchen with a delicious aroma. Every evening, the ritual was the same. The priest ladled the soup or the stew from the iron pot over the fire into two bowls. The first bowl he handed to the juggler. The second bowl he placed in front of his chair on the plain wooden table. Then he sat down, blessed the food, and the meal began. As the two men shared their supper, they unraveled their lives through the stories they shared.

"How did you become a priest in this parish?" asked the juggler one night.

"I hope you are enjoying your soup—it's a long story," said the old man. "You see, I was a very pious young man. I never focused my attention on this world. I thought the cares of this earth were insufficient to be worthy of my concern. I told everyone that my true purpose in life was to 'see' God and I spent my time thinking about God, reading about God, talking to God, and asking him to give me a sign of his presence. I wanted a miracle! My father figured I would never be of use to him or anybody else, so he sent me off to the monastery."

"The monastery must have been delighted to have such a devout person in their midst," exclaimed the juggler.

"Not exactly. The abbot was a very wise man. He felt that my quest for a miracle was selfish and my lofty concerns were haughty. The rhythm of monastery life includes contemplation, study, prayer, and hard work. The abbot felt that I needed a better understanding of the everyday world. He put me to work in the gardens with Brother Dominic."

"Is that why you have such an appreciation for gardening today?"

"Brother Dominic opened my eyes. Wonder permeated every moment he spent in the garden. Butterflies and hummingbirds, in particular, astonished him. Their delicate beauty and incredible endurance never failed to amaze him. He used to laugh aloud when he saw intoxicated bees emerge from flowers, covered in fuzzy, yellow nectar. Every spring, we planted rows and rows of seeds: peas, beans, and carrots. When they sprouted, he would turn to me and, in a hushed voice, say, "Look at that! Now we know that we are part of a bigger plan.'

"There wasn't much to do in the garden during the winter. During those months, the abbot put me to work in the kitchen helping Brother Alphonse. For him, hospitality was a sacred duty. He lovingly prepared every meal and offered it, as a gift, to his fellow monks. Strangers and travelers often sought refuge at our monastery. No one was ever turned away and Brother Alphonse welcomed everyone to his table."

"I am delighted with what you learned in the kitchen," said the juggler as he sipped his soup.

The old priest continued his story. "I had been at the monastery for about five years when an old friend of the abbot's came to visit. He was a priest in a small parish and was in need of help. The abbot assigned me to be his assistant. I stayed with the priest for two years, visiting the sick, caring for the poor, and lending a hand with the sacraments wherever I could. I began to see the grace of God as an intrinsic part of the daily lives of the people I served. It was in that little village that I discovered how I wanted to spend the rest of my life. I returned to the monastery, finished my studies, and was ordained a priest. I served in two other parishes before finally being sent here, and it is here that I have found my greatest happiness.

"And you?" asked the old priest. "How did you come to be a traveling juggler?"

"I guess you could say that I was born into it," explained the juggler. "You see, my mother and father belonged to a troupe of traveling players. At an early age, I learned how to juggle and perform a few simple balancing tricks. As I grew, it became evident that I possessed a natural ease and sense of balance. One of the acrobats in the company took me under his wing and taught me how to tumble and walk the rope. I loved everything about it: learning new routines, vaulting into the air, walking above the people. It was exhilarating and I felt so alive when I heard the exclamations and applause of the crowd."

"How wonderful to discover your gifts at such an early age."

"Maybe," said the juggler with a frown. "We were invited to perform in some of the finest houses and estates in the land. The audiences appreciated our talent and expertise. They paid us handsomely and lavished us with praise. But it did not last. Popularity is a fleeting thing. We understood our responsibility to our spectators. We practiced new techniques and kept our act fresh and lively, but despite our best efforts, after a few years we were no longer invited to the best places."

"What did you do?"

"At first, we tried to find fairs where we could work. But that wasn't enough. We traveled from town to town performing when people assembled on market day or when we could gather a few folks together in the village square. It was hard work and we barely earned enough for food and shelter. We couldn't afford new costumes or equipment. My mother took sick and died. Shortly afterward, my father died as well. The troupe disintegrated and I was forced to work alone."

The old priest set down his spoon and focused his attention on the young man. He noticed that the juggler's hand trembled slightly as he brought his spoon to his lips. "It must have been extremely difficult for you to be alone at such a young age," said the priest tenderly.

The juggler did not respond immediately. The old man's words unbound the ache that was festering in his heart. Haltingly, he released his sorrow. "I grew up surrounded by loving parents and companions who nurtured my spirit and encouraged my talent. One by one, they all disappeared. I remembered the joy I felt when spectators clapped and cheered in those fine houses where I performed as a boy, so I turned to my audiences for support. I performed my best routines in market squares and village halls, but the people who watched me gave only lukewarm responses. They seemed to have other things on their minds and I was, at best, a pleasant diversion. I stopped tumbling and returned to the predictable juggling tricks I learned as a child. They were adequate and enough to please the audience."

The priest nodded his head. "I understand," he replied. "You could not offer your true gifts to those who did not care."

The next morning, the two men busied themselves in the kitchen and prepared for the day ahead. They heard a timid knock at the back door. When the priest opened it, there stood the sad-eyed woman and her ragged little boy. She clutched her barren burlap sack anxiously in one hand and stammered a greeting to the priest. The old man invited her in. He reached up to grab his hat from the peg and spoke to the woman. "Why don't you let the little fellow stay in here and warm himself by the fire while we collect the vegetables." Turning to the juggler, he said, "I'm sure my friend here has a trick or two up his sleeve that will keep your boy amused." With that, he hurried the woman out the back door.

The juggler looked at the child's frightened face and gently patted the old chair next to the fireplace. The little boy cautiously climbed into it and let his spindly legs dangle toward the floor. The juggler smiled and, without a word, leaned over and picked up two spoons and a fork from the kitchen table. With a flourish, he tossed them into the air and began to juggle. The boy's eyes opened wide as he watched the circular trajectory of the sparkling silverware. The juggler added a cup and saucer to the circle of spinning cutlery and a smile broke through the curtain of fear that clouded the child's face. By the time the priest and the boy's mother returned, the child was utterly captivated by the juggler's tricks. When the woman saw her child's face, she stopped and her eyes filled with tears. "He seldom smiles at home," she said, and tentatively thanked the juggler. She took her son's hand and walked out the door. As he turned the corner, the little fellow looked back and gave a wave to the juggler.

When the winter winds began to blow, the juggler developed the habit of stopping by the church late in the afternoon, after his various tasks were completed. The peacefulness of the church comforted him;

he sat in a pew and let the stillness seep into his ragged soul. Sometimes, there were one or two other parishioners in the seats. More often, he sat alone. In the flickering light of the many candles that burned at her side, the juggler stared at the motionless statue of the Virgin with her Child balanced in the crook of her arm. She looked straight ahead, her unperturbed presence a sign of hope to all who lit a candle that their troubles and worries could not exhaust her serenity and strength.

As he sat in front of the Virgin's detached gaze, the fog of memory lifted and the past took form and shape in the juggler's thoughts. He remembered his mother's lullabies, his father's hearty laughter, and the guiding hand of the acrobat who had taught him to tumble. He recalled the first time he walked the tightrope and how happy he was when he heard the excited exclamations of surprise and delight from the audience below. The vividness of remembered joy was, at first, only a painful reminder of all that he had lost. During those quiet afternoons in front of the statue, the juggler sifted through the comings and goings of his past and found, in the recollections of happier times, a thin wisp of hope that his loneliness could change. The Virgin's accepting presence eased his pain, as if he no longer carried his burden alone, but shared it with another.

Snowflakes filled the sky and enveloped the countryside in a soft, white blanket of snow. Daylight faded early and the nights were long. The priest assembled the Advent wreath and placed it next to the altar, as a signal to the congregation that the season of waiting and preparation was at hand.

One evening the juggler remarked, "There's been a lot of activity in the church lately. More people are lighting candles, attending mass."

The old priest explained. "Christmas is coming. It is a very special time for our parish. As you know, the people have a special devotion to Our Lady. On Christmas Eve, there is a special midnight mass to celebrate the birth of the Christ Child. Afterward, there is a procession and people place gifts before the Virgin's statue, tokens of gratitude for Our Lady's abiding presence in the parish."

"What kind of gifts?"

"Well, some of the farmers cut the first few stalks of grain from their crops and save them for Our Lady. Their wives bundle them together with herbs from their gardens and tie them up with ribbons or weave them into small wreaths and place them before the statue. The cobbler often makes a special pair of shoes. The baker makes a loaf of holiday bread."

"What do you do with the gifts?" asked the juggler.

"I give the shoes to a parishioner who needs them. You and I will enjoy the bread."

When the juggler awoke the next day, he was still thinking about Christmas Eve. All morning long, as he chopped and stacked firewood, his thoughts returned to the procession after midnight Mass. He recalled those long afternoons when he sat under the watchful gaze of the wooden statue, pondering his life, and the gradual lightening of the weight of his memories. He wanted to acknowledge the Virgin's unwavering steadfastness. That afternoon, as he stared at the stoic face of the Lady who embraced the sorrows of the parish, the juggler realized what he wanted to do.

The juggler left the church and strode to an empty stall in the cowshed. With his foot, he quickly brushed aside the straw that covered the dirt floor. Slowly, he stretched his arms and legs, reaching upward and out, flexing and loosening unused muscles. He took a deep breath, closed his eyes for a moment and then somersaulted across the floor. He stood up and smiled to himself. Then he leaned forward, tumbled into a handstand and executed a back flip that became a rolling cartwheel. His first few turns were guarded, but his body quickly recovered its old rhythm, and his leaps became a graceful dance around the stall. Unaware of the fading daylight, the juggler continued tumbling until the evening star appeared in the blue-edged night sky.

As Christmas drew closer, a sense of anticipation permeated the parish. One morning, the juggler stood in the center aisle of the church and looked around at the stark, stone interior. When the priest entered, the juggler called out to him and said, "I think the church could use some sprucing up. It looks a little dreary and I would be glad to dress it up for midnight Mass."

"What a gracious offer," replied the priest. "I gladly accept." The juggler bustled about in an energetic flurry. Broom in hand, he swept the church from top to bottom, removing the dirt from the floor and cobwebs from the rafters. He made several trips into the woods and returned with armloads of pine boughs and cedar branches, which he stacked at the back of the church. When his chores were finished in the late afternoon, he crept into the cowshed and honed his routine into an elegant ballet of leaps and turns.

The day before Christmas, the juggler decorated the church. He tied evergreens with red ribbons, placed them on the windowsills, and set beeswax candles in their midst. He climbed onto a ladder and put cedar branches in the chandeliers and festooned the pillars with pine roping. All the while, he whistled happily to himself. When the priest entered the church and heard the happy sound, he looked up with a delighted grin and remarked, "You seem to be infected with the joy of the season. It's a pleasure to hear."

The juggler stopped for a moment and became aware of the eagerness that he felt. "I'm looking forward to tonight's celebration," he said.

Christmas Eve arrived. The stars pricked holes in the blackened night and allowed the hidden wonder of the heavens to shine through. Inside the tiny church, candles twinkled in a glittering replica of the night sky. With a satisfied smile, the juggler looked around and admired his handiwork. At half past eleven, he grabbed hold of the thick bell rope, gave it a tug, and the chimes of the church bells beckoned the villagers to midnight Mass. As the townsfolk waited for the mass to start, they fidgeted in their seats and chattered to each other in excited whispers. Wearing elegant vestments shot through with gold and green threads, the old priest entered the sanctuary and summoned the people to prayer. They rose to their feet and responded to his call, their voices reverberating through the church with a tingling sense of anticipation.

When the Mass was over, the priest uttered an eloquent prayer to Our Lady and invited the people to come forward. One by one, they left the pews and proceeded up the center aisle, carrying their gifts, offerings of thanks and praise harvested from the efforts of their daily lives. The worried woman in her faded red shawl knelt and placed before the statue a small braid of hand-dyed yarn. The little boy who regularly visited the rectory with his mother had collected small pinecones and tied them to a willow branch that he formed into a delicate wreath. There were loaves of bread, jars of jam, and a small, yellow cheese.

The juggler awaited his turn. Finally, he stepped out of the shadows and stood behind the others. He could feel the puzzled stares of the congregants as they watched him walk up the aisle empty-handed. At last, he stood before the Virgin and her Child. He gave a bow and then, bending low, cartwheeled across the floor. The old priest sat in his chair on the altar and watched the juggler as he tumbled and vaulted. A look of serenity came over the young man and he was no longer aware of his physical surroundings; his pulse connected to a rhythm beyond himself. He stood on his hands and flipped backward as if his body were as light as a feather. At first, the parishioners were shocked. "What is he doing?" they gasped. "This sort of thing belongs on the street, not here in the church!" However, as the juggler continued to leap and spring about, his body an elegant comma stroke swirling through air, the faces of the people became transfixed in wonder.

All of a sudden, a little boy shouted out, "Look, look! Our Lady … she is smiling." Everyone turned to look at the statue. The grave, wooden angles of the Virgin's face had softened into gentle contours. Her cheeks had inflated into soft pillows that pulled the corners of her mouth into a broad smile. As she stared directly at the juggler, the corners of her eyes crinkled with delight. She was smiling! The juggler was so absorbed in what he was doing that, at first, he was unaware of what had happened. The old priest left his chair and stood quietly next to him. Feeling the priest's presence, the juggler stopped and straightened himself.

The old man placed his hand on the juggler's shoulder and pointed toward the statue. "Look," he said. "Your gift has made Our Lady smile." The juggler gaped in amazement at the Lady, unable to speak. Then the priest gestured toward the villagers. "My son, look at their faces. It is a miracle! A miracle for us all." The young juggler saw the faces of the townsfolk, wrapped in joy. A tear trickled down his cheek as he whispered a thank-you to those in front and then turned to Our Lady and bowed low.

The smile remained on the statue's face, a welcome sign of Our Lady's compassion. Soon the little church became known as the Chapel of the Smiling Virgin. The juggler found work with a troupe of traveling actors and acrobats. However, every Christmas he returned to the little village and at Christmas Eve Mass, he vaulted and tumbled for Our Lady and all the parishioners of that tiny church.

The everyday world can take our breath away. The improbable flight of hummingbirds, the beauty of sunlight dancing across the water, the minute perfection of a newborn's hands and feet cause us to pause in awe and marvel at the wonders of creation. We touch upon mystery and suspect there is something beyond what we see. The Hebrew word for miracle is nes, *which also means a "sign." A miracle is a suspension of the natural order of things, an impossible happening that can only be explained by divine intervention.*

This repositioning of things opens up a new awareness. The significance of the miracle is more than the extraordinary completion of a specific feat. A miracle is revelatory; it points to the order of things beyond ordinary appearances and expands our grasp of reality. Miracles offer an invitation to take what we see through the fleeting shift in the temporal order and integrate this new knowledge into our everyday lives. That is the true nature of miracle—a change of heart.

6

The Magic Paintbrush

A Chinese Tale Retold

The artist Wang Fu received his magic paintbrush from the dragon of the mountains, who breathed forth a shower of mist onto Wang Fu as he slept underneath the sheltering branches of a juniper tree. In his dream, Wang Fu saw the moss-colored dragon slip out of a cave in a tall, craggy mountain and glide toward him. The tender, warm mist of the dragon's breath enveloped him, and Wang Fu knew that the watery vapor cloaked a rare and wonderful gift. Wang Fu opened his eyes. At first he could see nothing through the swaddling fog but, slowly, the hazy veil parted to reveal the dragon's offering. On top of a rock lay an exquisite paintbrush. Its handle was made of raindrop bamboo and it had long white bristles from the beard of a mountain goat.

Wang Fu sat unmoving with his back against the juniper tree and pondered the significance of the brush before him. He turned his gaze toward the mountain spires and bowed to the dragon concealed within them, his head touching the moist earth. When he sat upright, droplets of water anointed his forehead. Wang Fu reached out and with his right hand embraced the handle of the brush.

Wang Fu reverently positioned his footsteps on the path and slowly walked back to his studio. He stretched out a length of silk, tentatively dipped his brush into a pot of ink, and began to paint. Effortlessly the brush slid across the smooth surface, generating delicate strokes of light and shadow. The lines yielded the form and essence of the trees and hillsides, rocks and waterfalls. Never before had Wang Fu been able to paint with such grace and elegance.

One day Wang Fu gathered up his magic brush, his ink, and some paper and stepped outdoors. A little pool of water underneath a lone pine tree captured his attention. The dappled sunlight created subtle shadows that floated on the water's surface. Fascinated, Wang Fu watched as the fish in the pond darted in and out of those shadows. He took out his brush and became so absorbed in painting that he did not notice the minutes as they flowed by. When Wang Fu felt his wet robe clutching his ankles, he looked down and saw that he was standing in the pool of water. The paper had dissolved and the tip of his brush stroked the scales of a wriggling carp. Wang Fu's painting had sprung to life.

With a yelp, Wang Fu pulled back his brush and jumped out of the water. He grabbed the rest of his paper and ink and ran back to the confines of his studio. Wang Fu stared at the brush in his trembling hand. For the first time, he understood its power and potential; this paintbrush could bring things to life. Overwhelmed by such responsibility, Wang Fu resolved, from that moment forward, to practice restraint. His paintings became marvelous depictions of the world around him, but never again did they shimmer to life.

A provincial official from the court of a wealthy landlord happened to pass by the open door of Wang Fu's studio one afternoon. He stood outside and watched as Wang Fu's brush washed ink across the paper, making a regal mountain appear. "That painting is wonderful," he complimented Wang Fu. "May I see more?"

Wang Fu invited him in. With the shyness of a maiden on her wedding night, he untied several silk scrolls and uncovered his paintings.

"My master must see these," marveled the official. Wang Fu bundled up several scrolls and followed the servant to the magnificent residence of the wealthy landlord.

One by one, the landlord examined the landscapes. The contours of his face wore alternate expressions of delight, melancholy, and reverence. He raised his head and spoke wistfully to Wang Fu. "I long to wander along forest paths, listening to the song of finches and the babble of mountain streams, but I cannot. I must spend all my time tending to matters of my property and tenants. When I look at your paintings I feel as if I am in the very places you have drawn. Wang Fu, you can bring the outside world to me. Will you paint for me?"

Wang Fu returned to his little studio, collected his ink, paper, and scrolls of silk, and moved into the lord's manor, establishing himself as the official painter for the court. In all kinds of weather, during every season, he roamed the countryside observing the intimate details of the landscape and faithfully carrying the memories back home. With his magic brush, he painted the seductive lightness of rippling brooks as well as the tragic power of stooped juniper trees. The boundary between the physical structure of the house and the natural world beyond gradually softened, as Wang Fu's marvelous paintings enlivened every wall of that great house.

When gray hairs covered Wang Fu's head, he realized that with his death, the magic paintbrush would be lost forever, and he began to think of passing it on to someone else. He searched the nearby towns and villages looking for a suitable candidate. As he strolled along the riverbank early one morning, he noticed the silhouette of a boy skipping along the beach, trailing a stick in the sand. Upon closer inspection, Wang Fu realized that the boy was not skipping; he was drawing. Every line in the mud extended into a rhythmic flourish in his body. As he worked, he danced along the shore.

Suddenly, as if an invisible hand had jerked him from his reverie, the boy dropped his stick and began to collect pieces of driftwood. Wang Fu studied what the boy had drawn. Even in the sand, his delicate lines had captured the essence of the reeds swaying in the breeze to an unheard tempo and the raindrops capering on the water's surface in tiny little circles. Wang Fu walked up to the boy. "I see that you like to draw," he said.

A wide smile stretched across the boy's face as he replied, "Yes, whenever I can. Sometimes I use a stick, sometimes a piece of charcoal if I can spare it. Sometimes I just dip my finger in the water and paint on rocks." A tone of longing crept into his voice. "If only I had a brush. Who knows what I could do?"

Wang Fu considered the boy in front of him. His scraggy frame held up rags and tatters that passed for clothes, making him look much younger than he was. However, his scrawny body and worn-out clothes could not diminish his exuberance. Wang Fu made a decision. "My name is Wang Fu. I am a painter. I have brushes and ink and paper. Meet me here tomorrow and I will show you how to use them," he said.

The boy's voice quivered with excitement. "Really? You will teach me to paint?" Wang Fu nodded solemnly. "Oh, thank you. I will be here tomorrow morning, early. But now I have to go and sell this firewood or I won't be able to eat tonight." He bent down to retrieve the bundle of sticks and twigs at his feet. He started to walk away. As an afterthought, he turned back and called out, "My name is Ma Liang."

The next morning, Wang Fu assembled his paper, ink, and brushes on a large flat rock by the river's edge. When Ma Liang arrived, he showed him a few simple techniques and then handed the boy a brush. Eagerly, Ma Liang plucked the brush from his hand, dipped it into the ink, and began to paint. His hand moved with a natural ease. He twirled the brush across the paper, twisting and swirling it with subtle agility. Wang Fu observed Ma Liang intently. The boy had an innate sense of balance as well as an imaginative eye. When he was finished, Wang Fu examined Ma Liang's work. He was amazed at what he saw. Simply and without pretense, Ma Liang had sketched a rocky mountain clothed in trees. The clean lines eloquently expressed the hidden order beneath the surface of things.

Ma Liang became Wang Fu's apprentice. Every two weeks, Wang Fu would visit Ma Liang's humble reed hut. He showed him how to mix the ink with mineral pigments, how to control the brush and make strokes that moved from dark to light, solid to hollow. Wang Fu recognized Ma Liang's aptitude and encouraged his gift. He provided Ma Liang with all the necessary tools of his craft. Aware that the boy spent long hours gathering and selling firewood as his livelihood, Wang Fu gave him money so that he could spend time painting and still have food to eat.

As Wang Fu nurtured Ma Liang's talent, he discovered that the boy's artistry reflected a passionate spirit that delighted in the wonder of the world around him. Ma Liang's paintings were more than vivid evocations of particular places. He set forth his heart on the paper and revealed his innate goodness with every brushstroke. Wang Fu was reticent by nature and seldom dipped into the well of his emotions. His elegant lines formed landscapes that remarkably portrayed the place itself, but his personality never emerged on his silken scrolls.

In the slanting sunlight of an autumn afternoon, Ma Liang painted a willow tree with such sincerity that Wang Fu mourned the fluttering sadness of the leaves on the weeping branches. Hesitantly, Wang Fu tried to explain his feelings. Ma Liang listened intently to his words. When Wang Fu finished speaking, Ma Liang shared the story of his parents' death and told his teacher of the sadness he carried in his heart. As the days passed, Wang Fu's fondness for the boy grew. He spent less and less time working in his studio in the mansion and more time teaching his young protégé.

The boy's dedication and capability impressed Wang Fu, and he was eager to give Ma Liang the magic paintbrush. Nevertheless, Wang Fu worried that the boy could not fully appreciate the brush's possibilities. Wang Fu decided to stay with Ma Liang to give him guidance and a helping hand. Wang Fu gathered a few personal necessities and several strings of coins from his rooms in the manor house. He carefully wrapped the magic paintbrush in red silk and tied the package with golden thread. Then Wang Fu stepped out of his room, closed the door behind him, and shrugged off his old life like a robe at the end of a long day.

Wang Fu arrived at Ma Liang's tiny house just as the sun pulled its last ray above the horizon. He took the crimson package in his hands and presented it to Ma Liang. "The dragon of the mountains gave me this long ago. It has helped me to see the beauty of this world and share it with others." Ma Liang took the parcel and unwrapped it. Wang Fu cautioned him, "It is a magic paintbrush. It has the power to bring your painting to life. Use it wisely, Ma Liang."

Ma Liang reverently lifted the magnificent brush from the scarlet silk. His fingers gripped the handle and he spoke in a voice that trembled with gratitude. "Thank you, my dearest Wang Fu. I will do my best to honor your trust."

Ma Liang did not hesitate. He took out a pot of ink and began to paint. Ma Liang reveled at the ease with which the brush slipped across the silk, his brushstrokes filling the canvas with lyric elegance. A finch settled on a pine branch outside Ma Liang's window and began to warble. The bird's melodious chirping captivated Ma Liang and he traced its outline onto the paper. Wang Fu watched as the boy worked. His face took on an expression of rapt attention. Soon, the paper wriggled and a little wing began to flap upward. A tiny brown bird fluttered off the paper and flitted about the room. When Ma Liang realized what had happened, he threw back his head and laughed with delight. He turned to Wang Fu and exclaimed, "What a wonderful gift!"

As Ma Liang sat in front of his house drawing a lazy cat dozing in the sun, his neighbor looked over and began to watch him. Ma Liang worked so intently that he was unaware of the man's curious gaze. Suddenly, a cat jumped off Ma Liang's paper, scampered into the grass and came out, holding a twitching mouse in its teeth. The neighbor gasped in surprise and ran toward Ma Liang. "How did you do that?" he exclaimed. Ma Liang's mouth gaped open. He did not know what to say.

Wang Fu, who had seen everything, intervened. "Ah, it was nothing. The cat was merely hiding underneath Ma Liang's paper. When it saw the mouse, it jumped up. I know it looked as if Ma Liang had painted it to life, but how could such a thing be? It is impossible." The neighbor, not totally convinced by Wang Fu's story, laughed nervously and returned home.

Wang Fu turned to Ma Liang. He was concerned that the boy's fervor would lead to recklessness. He gazed at Ma Liang's innocent face and chided him gently. "Your enthusiasm has run ahead of you. You must protect your gift. Do not squander the magic of the brush. Be careful, Ma Liang, careful of yourself and careful of others!"

Ma Liang heeded Wang Fu's warning. He learned to discipline himself and remain watchful of his thoughts so that he did not become entranced unnecessarily. However, Ma Liang could not safeguard his kind heart. One day, his neighbor returned. "Ma Liang, my ox has died. Without that ox, I cannot tend my fields and my family will have nothing to eat. Please, Ma Liang, can you paint me an ox that will come to life?" he implored.

The desperate sound of the man's voice touched those still-tender memories of nights when Ma Liang had gone to bed hungry. He could not ignore his neighbor's plea. Ma Liang picked up his magic paintbrush and brought forth a fine, healthy ox. "Thank you, Ma Liang. You have saved my family from starvation," said the man.

Ma Liang immediately went to Wang Fu and confessed the details of the incident. "Wang Fu, the magic possibility of this brush cannot remain hidden. I must use it to help those in need."

Although Ma Liang asked his neighbor not to tell anyone what had happened, word slipped out about his magic paintbrush. Soon, there were other requests from people in Ma Liang's village. The people had grown accustomed to a life that offered no shelter from hardship. They came to Ma Liang only when they could find no other way out of their difficulties. "Please, Ma Liang," petitioned a widow with five children, "will you paint me a flock of chickens so that my children can eat?" An old man bent over with age asked Ma Liang to paint him a cane. Ma Liang honored their humble requests. He even tried to relieve their sorrows. One day he found a little boy crying at the roadside because his grandmother was dying. Ma Liang visited her deathbed and with his brush fashioned a cloud of rainbow-colored butterflies that flitted about the room and eased her suffering.

The mysterious power of Ma Liang's brush filled the villagers with wonder and admiration. They were grateful for Ma Liang's generosity and respectfully honored his request to keep silent about the magic paintbrush. However, one of the villagers, a man by the name of Chen Lin, journeyed to a neighboring province to visit his cousin. The two men had not seen each other for some time. At first they talked about trivial matters and family gossip. As the night wore on, their conversation turned to issues of greater importance, and they discussed their hopes, dreams, fears, and the things of this world that bewildered them. The awesome power of Ma Liang's paintbrush had always perplexed Chen Lin. He shared his puzzlement with his cousin and told him about Ma Liang, Wang Fu, and the magic in the paintbrush. Astonished by Chen Lin's amazing story, his cousin told everyone he knew.

Soon, the governor-general of that province heard about Ma Liang's brush. He ordered his servants to find Ma Liang. "Bring him to me," commanded the governor-general. "I would like to see for myself if there is magic in that peasant's paintbrush. With such power, I could have anything I want."

A week later, Ma Liang, accompanied by Wang Fu and two provincial officials, trudged along a steep path that led to the governor-general's palace on a rocky outcropping halfway up the mountainside. The officials escorted Ma Liang and Wang Fu into a large, dimly lit room. Encircled by the soft glow of candles, the governor-general was ensconced in a large chair ornately carved in the shape of a dragon. A long, wispy mustache framed his thin lips. He hissed a greeting to Ma Liang and his teacher.

"Welcome, gentlemen. You must be tired after your long journey. Rest and I will have tea brought out." The governor-general chatted pleasantly until they finished their tea. Then he leaned over on one arm, grasped the chair with his bony hand, and looked directly at Ma Liang. "It has come to my attention that you have a paintbrush that can bring things to life. Is that true?"

"Yes," said Ma Liang hesitantly.

"I would like to see how it works. Won't you paint something for me, Ma Liang?"

"I only use the brush to help people in dire circumstances," explained Ma Liang resolutely. "I do not take its power casually."

The governor-general's eyes narrowed to small slits, but they did not blink. "How noble of you," he said. "I admire your restraint."

The governor-general recognized Ma Liang's tenacity. He knew he could not persuade Ma Liang to use that brush for his own purposes, so he decided to steal it. That night as Ma Liang and Wang Fu lay sleeping, one of the governor-general's officials made his way into their bedchamber and tiptoed through the darkness looking for the brush. Wang Fu slept lightly, and when he heard the intruder's velvety footsteps, he opened his eyes and saw the thief creeping through the shadows. Wang Fu smiled to himself. Feigning a nightmare, he began to scream and thrash about. The burglar quickly departed.

When Ma Liang heard Wang Fu's shrieks, he sat bolt upright. Wang Fu explained what had happened. "We need to leave this place at once," he declared. They escaped through the gloomy corridors of the palace and fled into the ink-black night. When the pale dawn brightened into early morning, two soldiers on horseback overtook Ma Liang and Wang Fu, bound their wrists, and brought them back to the governor-general's stronghold.

"Ah, Ma Liang," chuckled the governor-general. "Did you really think I would let you and that magic brush out of my grasp?" The governor-general motioned toward a large silk screen that stood on the floor. "Ma Liang, I would like you to paint a dragon for me, a dragon that will bring me good luck. If you do not paint for me, then your old teacher will lose his head." As he said those words, the governor-general gave a curt nod and two swordsmen stepped forward. Each one placed a meaty fist around Wang Fu's arm and held him tightly.

Ma Liang did not hesitate. He marched up to the screen, took out his ink and brush, and began to paint. Deliberately, he placed strong, bold strokes onto the canvas. The governor-general watched, fascinated, as Ma Liang leapt back and forth, pouring his energy onto the screen, filling it with the formidable figure of a mighty dragon. The screen shuddered and wobbled. With a violent quake, a powerful dragon covered in cobalt scales jumped out of the screen and planted its taloned feet onto the floor. Expectantly, the governor-general stood up. His thin lips stretched into a smug grin. The dragon extended to its full height and spread its silvery wings until they encompassed the entire room. Its pointed tail twitched and rasped across the floorboards. The governor-general's eyes widened with awe. The dragon's cavernous mouth yawned wide-open and with a deafening roar emitted an ominous gray cloud. Thunder clapped, lightning flashed, and a driving sheet of rainwater spilled out of that cloud. As the rain poured down, the water level in the room rose higher and higher. The governor-general cried out in panic. The swordsmen loosened their grip on Wang Fu as they began to paddle about, seeking safety from the rising flood.

The dragon bent low and with its forefeet gently scooped Ma Liang and Wang Fu out of the swirling water. The waters raged with such force that the walls of that room splintered and the entire palace collapsed. The governor-general and his officials cascaded down the mountainside in a torrent of water and debris. Protected in the dragon's cupped feet, Ma Liang and Wang Fu soared up through the storm cloud as the dragon flapped its great wings and carried them to safety. Up and up they flew. Ma Liang and Wang Fu peered over the dragon's scaly claws at the chaos below. Eventually, the gray cloud, the ruined palace, and its inhabitants disappeared from sight. The dragon gently deposited the artist and his teacher on a mountaintop near a grove of pine trees. Ma Liang still clenched the magic paintbrush in his fist. The two men gazed into the dragon's deep yellow eyes and together, in a gesture of gratitude, they bowed low. The dragon exhaled and enveloped Ma Liang and Wang Fu in a shimmering, thick fog. When the mist cleared, the dragon was gone.

Ma Liang and Wang Fu did not return to the village. The villagers began to wonder what had happened to them. However, stories began to reach the village about a young artist and his old teacher who traveled the countryside helping those in need with a marvelous, magical paintbrush that made pictures come to life. At first, the villagers sorely missed Ma Liang, but as more and more people explained how Ma Liang had changed their lives, they realized that his gift was too important to be contained by the needs of their little village. They began to take pride in Ma Liang's accomplishments. Whenever travelers came to their town, they delighted in telling them the story of Ma Liang and how he had used his magic brush for the first time in their village.

The Old French word miracle *derives from the Latin* miraculum, *meaning "object of wonder." Artists possess a craving for beauty that predisposes them toward miracles; the everyday world becomes suffused with wonder and they marvel at what they see. Artists take in this sensory data, give it time to settle, to brush up against the mystery of the mind and the heart, then shape and redefine it until a new image is formed. The act of imagining, which allows a new image to surface subtly, changes the artists as well. Their perspective shifts, new insights are gained, and they understand the world in a slightly different way.*

The experience of beauty absorbs and enlivens us. We bring ourselves to a work of art—our emotions, our memories, and our sense of the way things work. We respond to the vision of the artist and see our lives reflected back to us in a new way. The poem, the story, the painting becomes a container for our thoughts and feelings; we are drawn out of the narrow concerns of our personal lives and pulled into a new world that expands our awareness, awakens us to the deeper significance of life, and allows us to see beyond appearances into spirit.

7

A Dream for Ruth

An English Folktale Retold

Ruth poured the boiling water from the whistling teakettle into her cup, walked out the back door, and headed toward the weeping willow by the river's edge. She had always done her best thinking underneath that tree. Ruth parted the curtain of trailing branches and settled herself onto the old wooden bench worn smooth with years of use. Placing her china cup on the weathered table, she tried to unravel the meaning of last night's puzzling dream. Ruth had dreamed that her mother was standing at the foot of her bed, her long silver hair twisted into a bun at the back of her neck. She was standing straight and tall and called out in a strong voice, "Ruth, listen to me. Get up out of bed. Walk to the town with the red sandstone church. Stand on the bridge. Listen, Ruth, and you will hear a voice that will tell you of a great treasure. Get up, Ruth, and go!" Ruth had awakened with such a strong feeling of her mother's presence that when she walked out of her bedroom, she half expected to see her mother sitting at the kitchen table.

As she sipped her hot water, Ruth could picture the town with the red sandstone church. When she was about ten years old, she had visited that place with her father and had marveled at the busy streets and lively people. Her father had set aside a little money so that he and

Ruth could share a sandwich and a piece of pie at a local diner; Ruth had never eaten in a restaurant before. However, no matter how hard she tried, Ruth could not recollect how to get back to that town.

"Whose voice am I going to hear? What kind of treasure? What does it all mean?" she whispered aloud, shaking her head back and forth.

A gentle breeze stirred, causing the willow branches to sway slightly and release a few golden, tear-shaped leaves into the river. As Ruth watched the delicate leaves drift by, swirling and twirling on the surface of the water, memories emerged and the whole course of her life seemed to flow before her.

Life had not been easy in that little brown cabin. As a child, Ruth was not aware of the difficulties; her parents had a knack for accepting whatever the world offered them and creating a life filled with beauty and wonder, a talent they passed on to their daughter. Ruth's mother foraged in the woods for mushrooms, nuts, berries, and wild honey to add flavor and interest to food that was otherwise plain and simple. She transplanted wildflowers around the cabin, wove baskets out of grapevines, and filled the house with wooden angels fashioned from twigs and bark. Ruth followed behind her as she worked and listened as her mother told her stories about woodland creatures, hidden treasures, and animals that danced and sang.

Ruth's father was a handyman who did odd jobs for the people in town. From late spring to early autumn, he would pack up his tools each day and walk almost two hours into town to earn the few dollars that provided his family with the things they could not make or find. He had a group of regular customers who liked his work and trusted him. In addition to his wages, they often sent him home with a little extra something for his family—tomatoes from the garden, fresh eggs from the henhouse, a bag of apples from the orchard. In the winter months, when the forest path was impassable due to snow, he repaired old furniture and constructed benches and birdhouses from scraps of lumber.

Ruth had no brothers and sisters, no nearby friends or neighbors to pass the time with, but she was seldom lonely. She peopled her days with characters from her mother's stories, acting out adventures in the clearing around her house. Her favorite place to play was underneath the weeping willow tree where the cascading branches surrounded her with a delicate canopy. She listened to the river rush over the rocks and entered an imaginary world where anything was possible.

One summer night as Ruth's father sat eating his warmed-over supper, he regaled Ruth and her mother with stories about the people he worked for in town. Fascinated by her father's adventures, Ruth begged to go with him. At the young age of five, she began to accompany him periodically. Using scraps of lumber, discarded machinery parts, and old bicycle tires, he built a wagon. He piled his tools into the wagon and, holding Ruth's tiny hand in his big one, hiked into town. When Ruth grew tired, he plopped her into the wagon alongside the tools. The townsfolk soon became accustomed to the sight of Ruth's father, whistling as he walked along, pulling a makeshift wagon with a smiling little girl leaning over the sides.

Ruth became acquainted with many of her father's patrons. Mrs. Fullerton was a retired librarian. As Ruth's father repaired her front porch, she taught Ruth how to read, sending her home each week with a new book. When the autumn winds blew cold, she packed up several volumes, including a thick copy of Hans Christian Andersen's fairy tales, and handed them to Ruth. "Take these," she said. "They'll help you get through the long winter."

Throughout the winter, those books became Ruth's companions. While her parents slept, she turned up the wick on her lamp and read late into the night. She fell asleep staring out the window at the stars twinkling through the trees. In her dreams, Ruth saw a fairy flittering through the moonlit night, hanging the stars from tree branches. Each star contained a child's wish and the fairy made the forest promise to safeguard the hopes and dreams inside the stars.

The year that Ruth turned thirteen, a no-nonsense widow named Shirley purchased a large two-story brick house in town. She planned to rent out rooms to summer visitors and hired Ruth's father to help her fix up the building. Ruth had learned enough about carpentry to assist her father, and came into town with him every day. Impressed with Ruth's ability, Shirley offered her a job. For the next two summers, Ruth worked at Shirley's Inn, serving breakfast, making beds, and tending the garden. Shirley had no children of her own and treated Ruth like a daughter. On warm summer evenings, when the day's work was finished, they would sit on the back porch steps as Shirley plaited Ruth's long, black hair into two thick braids. The two of them laughed and chatted about the interesting lives and the idiosyncratic habits of the clients who stayed at the inn.

Toward the end of her second summer at Shirley's, Ruth's mother became ill and Ruth returned home to care for her. Two years later, her father developed heart problems and could no longer work. Faced with the care of two invalid parents, Ruth needed to find a way to earn money. Resourcefulness and determination were ingrained in Ruth. One afternoon, as she sat underneath the weeping willow, watching the tiny leaves flutter in the breeze, an idea took shape in her mind.

Ruth pulled out a big box of empty wooden spools from her father's workshop. She gathered scraps of fabric, bits of yarn and thread, tiny pinecones from the hemlock tree, and piled everything on the back porch. She stitched and snipped, getting up extra early in the morning and staying up late at night, to complete her project. After three weeks, she created, from leftover this and that, two dozen angel dolls, complete with patchwork wings and tiny pinecone halos.

She packed them up, brought them to Shirley, and asked if her summer guests might be interested in purchasing the dolls. Within an hour, she sold three of them. Ruth called on a few of Shirley's friends and was able to sell four more dolls. Shirley took the rest on consignment. Before she left town that afternoon, Ruth had earned enough money to buy a month's worth of supplies and had discovered a direction forged from necessity that would shape the rest of her life.

Over the next few years, Ruth produced a variety of creations, unraveling sweaters, unstitching old quilts, rummaging through her house and the forest for raw materials. She made things not only to earn money, but also to ease the troubles and bring delight into the lives of those she met. From a pile of discarded wood scraps, she had created birdhouses for Mrs. Molnar, a widow who lived all by herself in an ancient rambling house with a big backyard. When the old woman put them atop the fenceposts in her backyard to attract the birds, the flittering creatures provided her with company and lightened her spirits.

After buying a set of Ruth's lace place mats, her customer Mrs. McCarthy had said, "Ruth, our church is looking worn and dreary. The people are tired out. Even our pastor is running out of enthusiasm. We need a touch of beauty to soften the harshness of our days. Ruth, I was wondering, could you make an altar cloth like one of these place mats?"

It took Ruth three weeks, working from early morning till late at night, to complete the altar cloth, made from the unraveled thread of an old crocheted bedspread. She delivered it to Mrs. McCarthy with a posy of wildflowers tucked into its graceful folds. "Why, Ruth," declared Mrs. McCarthy as she lifted the cloth toward the window, allowing the light to reveal the fine, intricate stitches, "it's exquisite. I've never seen anything so lovely." In Mrs. McCarthy's hands, the cloth took on special significance, her acknowledgment of its beauty pronouncing its worth and affirming Ruth's individuality, her gift, her artisanship.

Ruth's days took on an added richness; her plans and offerings connected her to a community beyond the concerns and cares of her tiny household. When her parents died, she remained in the rustic cabin, sheltered by the forest with its lone weeping willow tree and sustained by her familiar routine.

However, the past few years had been particularly difficult. The town seemed to grow thinner with every visit. People moved away or died, businesses failed, and no one moved in to replace them. Even Shirley had closed her inn, moving away to live with her brother in the city. Abandoned buildings lined the streets, the paint flaking from their withered exteriors, broken windows revealing empty rooms. All that remained was a gaunt skeleton of the place. Ruth's regular circle of customers shrank and those who stayed found it harder and harder to scrape together enough coins to afford the things that Ruth sold. In order to make ends meet, she had sold her great-aunt's clock and her father's tools. She had even disassembled her mother's satin wedding dress, meticulously cutting the satin and lace into smaller pieces and fashioning them into Christmas angels. She saved a few remnants and made herself an ornate pillow that she placed on her bed. The only other treasures she held onto were her books and her grandmother's china cups and saucers.

Stripped of all but the essentials, Ruth's cabin no longer afforded her the resources for creativity. She managed to stretch out her rations until late autumn but finally there was nothing left in her cupboards, and Ruth was forced to go to bed hungry. That night, her mother had appeared to her in the dream. Now, as she sat underneath the willow tree in the chilly autumn air, sipping hot water from a china cup, she tried to piece together a plan. All day long, she mulled over her mother's words but the promise held out in her dream seemed too fragile to pursue.

That night when she crawled into bed, Ruth once again dreamed about her mother and heard the same insistent plea. This time, however, as she tossed and turned, the dream continued. At first, images of houses, forests, and pathways were mixed up in a confusing jumble. After a while, a road became noticeable and Ruth saw herself walking along a definite route with distinct landmarks. At the end of the road, she saw the red sandstone church. When she awoke, Ruth was certain that she could find her way to the town she saw in her dream. In the clear light of day, though, her confidence began to falter. She wondered if walking to a strange town and waiting to learn about a mysterious treasure was a foolish thing to do. "But what have I got to lose?" she whispered to herself.

When Ruth heard her mother's command for the third night in a row, she sat straight up in bed and opened her eyes wide. In the faint light of dawn, she could make out the shape of things and slowly dressed herself. She boiled a cup of water and drank it down. Ruth put on an extra pair of socks, a heavy wool sweater, her father's long coat and gloves. She wrapped a scarf around her head, tied another about her neck, pulled up the collar of her coat. With a deep breath, she stepped out into the brisk December air. Snow had not yet fallen and the ground was bare. Ruth plodded along, doggedly putting one foot in front of the other, following the path she had seen in her dream. Her mother's words echoed in her ears and she whispered repeatedly, like a child reciting her prayers, "I'm on my way. I'm coming!" After several hours, she saw the steeple of the red sandstone church outlined against the pale winter sky. Ruth quickened her steps and made her way though the busy streets until she stood on the bridge.

The town was as lively as ever, with people bustling back and forth across the bridge and along the crowded streets. Ruth carefully watched their faces as they passed by, waiting for someone to recognize her and tell her about the treasure. She stayed on the bridge all day long, the cold wind whipping off the river and chilling her to the bone, but no one paid the slightest attention to her. It was as if she did not exist at all.

As the light of day waned, Ruth's hope faded and then disappeared completely when the deep blue of twilight arrived. Exhausted, cold, and hungry, she looked around in desperation. The only imaginable haven that presented itself was the red sandstone church. As Ruth started walking toward it, she heard a voice holler sharply, "Hey, you with the raggedy coat, wait up a minute." Ruth realized the person was shouting at her and turned around. A young woman wearing a white apron over a red-checked blouse ran up to her.

"Hey," she said, a little out of breath. "What is it with you? I've been watching you all day. You stood on this bridge for hours and never moved. What are you up to?"

Ruth opened her mouth to speak but could not find the right words. Bewildered, she just shook her head. The woman examined Ruth's haggard face. "You look just awful, honey!" she exclaimed. "Come with me." She took Ruth by the arm, led her into a cozy diner where the bridge met the main street, and sat her down in a booth near the kitchen. "You need something to eat," said the woman. "Something that will stick to your ribs. How about a bowl of bean soup to start with?"

Ruth nodded her head and the woman returned with a thick white bowl of soup in one hand and a steaming mug of coffee in the other. Ruth picked up a spoon in her gloved hand and began to eat ravenously. Slowly, her chilled body responded to the warmth of the soup, the coffee, and the woman's hospitality. The numbness dissolved from Ruth's fingers and toes. She took off her gloves and unbuttoned her coat. The convivial chatter of the regulars penetrated her frozen stupor, and she lifted her head to smile at the woman.

"Thank you," she said. "What is your name?"

"Martha. And you're welcome. What's your name?"

"Ruth—nice to meet you." Ruth extended her hand across the table. Martha clasped Ruth's bony fingers gently.

"You're as thin as a piece of paper," she said. "How about a sandwich to go with that soup?"

"That would be perfect," said Ruth. Martha brought her a grilled cheese sandwich, fried potatoes, and a big piece of lemon meringue pie. As Martha bustled about serving her customers, Ruth ate silently, completely absorbed by the taste and smell of her meal.

When Ruth had finished, Martha sat down and, looking her right in the eye, said, "Now that you're fed, can you please tell me what you're up to?"

Ruth was unsure of where to begin. Confronted with Martha's straightforward manner, Ruth felt a little foolish explaining her quest.

"I had a dream," she said.

"What?" Martha cocked her head to one side and twisted her face into a quizzical expression.

"I had the same dream three times. In it I saw the red sandstone church and the bridge. I'm sure it was a sign. I had no choice but to follow it."

"Well, I give you credit, honey," said Martha, shaking her head and grinning in disbelief. "I have dreams, too, but I don't follow them. I've got responsibilities. I stay put and keep an eye on the here and now." She paused. "But you know, I had a dream the other night. I dreamt that I saw a tree, a strange sort of tree, with long dangly branches covered in thin leaves that flapped in the moonlight. Did you ever see anything like that?"

"It's called a weeping willow tree because the leaves look like tears falling off the branches. They grow near water. There aren't too many of them around here."

Martha continued. "Now, buried underneath this tree, there was a box, a big old tin box." Ruth leaned in closer.

"Was there anything in the box?" she asked.

"I don't know," chuckled Martha. "I woke up before I got to that part of the dream."

Ruth smiled at Martha. "Thanks for your kindness," she said. "I've got to get going—it will take me all night to get back home."

"Are you sure you're able to travel? You feel okay?"

"I'll be fine," said Ruth. "I feel a lot better now that I've eaten something. You're a lifesaver, Martha. You really are."

Martha patted Ruth's hand. "Okay, honey, you take care of yourself. You follow those dreams!"

Ruth hurried through the brightly lit streets until she came to the road that led back to her cabin. In the moonlight, she briskly retraced her steps along the pathway. Martha's words filled Ruth with determination; she was convinced that a box filled with treasure lay buried beneath the weeping willow tree. When Ruth saw her little cabin in the distance, she began to run.

Grabbing a shovel from her father's shed, she raced into the backyard and started to dig beneath the willow tree. A layer of frost covered the ground but it was not frozen and Ruth was able to dig without difficulty. Soon her shovel hit something hard. She scraped at it with her spade and saw a piece of metal poking through the earth. She continued digging, clearing away the soil until she uncovered the top of an old metal box, about three feet long and a foot wide. Finally, she was able to shove her spade beneath the chest and pry it loose from the earth. She tugged it out of the hole and knelt down in front of it. With her gloved hand, she swept away the dirt that still clung to the battered lid. Ruth reached out, her hands trembling, unfastened the clasp, and slowly lifted the lid.

Inside the chest was a collection of marvels. There were yards of richly patterned and wondrously colored fabric folded into neat squares. Next to the fabric, positioned in rows of tidy coils, were yards of rich lace and ornate trim. Ruth found three cigar boxes filled with thread of every color imaginable. There were jars of buttons and beads that sparkled like jewels in the moonlight, silver-colored thimbles, a tiny pair of embroidery scissors, and rolls and rolls of silk and satin ribbon. Ruth examined each and every thing in that chest, gasping with delight as she pulled out one treasure after another.

As she reached down to run her hand through some skeins of feathery yarn, Ruth felt a hard lump. She wriggled her fingers and pulled out a roll of paper money, wrapped in a rubber band. Ruth undid the roll and began to count the $5 and $10 bills. There was enough money to buy food for several years. Ruth threw back her head and, staring up at the heavens, shouted out as loud as she could, "Thank you, thank you, thank you!"

She closed the lid and dragged the old metal box into her cabin. Already her head was filled with plans. Tomorrow she would walk into town and buy enough food to last her for several months. Then she would spend the winter making things, things to brighten the days and lighten the burdens of all her friends in town.

As we sleep, our dreams unfold the jumbled panorama of the psyche. Dreams are sometimes seen as oracular visions, foretelling the future and advising us how to act. Dreams are also seen as a way for the psyche to work out the events and problems of the day, allowing the mind to uncover new solutions and possibilities. The images of the dream world are symbolic and, through careful interpretation, can give us clues about the journey of our lives.

Dreams also contain the potential that allows us to understand who we are as individuals. Each of our lives is made up of a variety of specific experiences that constitute our personal history. The images in our dreams often couple visual elements with intense emotions. These images have unique significance for each person, and exploring them in our waking hours can reveal a deeper awareness of who we are—creatively, emotionally, spiritually. Examining the peculiarities of our own dreamscapes can give us new perspective on past happenings and cultivate an appreciation for the distinctiveness of our own circumstances. Through our dreams, we expand our understanding of our own nature.

8

Stones and Treasures

A Jewish Folktale Retold

There was once a dreary little town filled with cantankerous people who complained all the time. The limestone buildings rubbed up against each other, their window slits looking out over narrow, pebbled streets. As the people shuffled through those streets, they kicked up dust that discolored their shoes and clung to the hems of their drab robes. Where the streets crossed, men stopped to gripe about the day's difficulties. "Another day, same as the one before," remarked one.

"Yes, work, work, work, nothing ever changes," replied another.

The women gathered at the well and groaned collectively. "Cook, cook, cook, clean, clean, clean, that's all we ever do. Does anyone notice? Certainly not! Our husbands never look beyond their own noses at us or at anything we do!"

The storekeepers stood in front of the shops that bordered the market square and lamented. "Look at this place, it is so dull. We have no mansions, no elegant buildings, no rich inhabitants to spend their money on our wares. The merchants from out of town never stay for more than a day." Even the children were restless and spent their time quarreling and whining.

The grumblings droned on until they arose, like a swarm of stinging gnats, into the heavens where God, who listens to prayer in all its

60

forms, heard the moans of those uneasy people. God called forth one of the angels and, pointing earthward, said, "Can you make out that dusty little town? The inhabitants have trouble seeing things clearly. Will you venture forth and help them?"

"I'll pay them a visit," promised the angel. "Perhaps I can provide a little illumination."

The next evening, as the sun languidly descended from the sky, a stranger arrived in the town. The day had been unusually hot, and the people were reclining in the shade of an enormous tree that grew in the center of the market square. The heat made them grouchier than usual and their faces were crumpled with irritability. Whistling softly, the stranger drifted out of one of the side streets and strolled toward the townsfolk. The threads of his silk clothing shimmered in the fading sunlight. One by one, the people stopped talking and gaped, open-mouthed, at the unusual fellow. He was quite unlike anyone they had ever seen. He wore a dazzling gold and blue tunic over crimson pants. Embroidered stars and moons danced across the toes of his purple velvet slippers. An effortless grace animated his movements and his gentle face crinkled with delight. At first, their eyes opened wide in amazement—but their gaze quickly narrowed with suspicion and their lips tightened warily.

"Who are you?" asked the mayor.

"Oh, I'm just a traveler," answered the stranger. "I wander here and there, taking in the sights and enjoying the company of those I meet along the way."

"Well, there isn't much to see here!" replied the mayor.

"How can you say that? Why, look at this magnificent tree. I have never seen a tree with such generous branches. And listen, the birds are gathering for the night. Their sweet song gladdens my heart."

"That squawking and screeching!" sputtered one of the merchants. "Why, it's nothing but noise. I can hardly hear myself think."

The stranger tilted his face upward and inhaled the aroma of evening meals that lingered in the warm air. "Cardamom and a hint of cloves," he observed. "What marvelous fragrances. Dinner must have been delicious tonight!"

"Soup and stew, stew and soup. It's all we ever have," complained the men.

The stranger surveyed the disgruntled townspeople and smiled ruefully. He turned his head and examined his surroundings. The setting sun suffused the town with a fiery apricot glow. The limestone faces of the buildings blushed ruddy gold and cast long, plum-colored shadows across the streets and onto shorter structures, forming a dramatic patchwork of light and dark. The stranger waved his hand in a delicate arc and pointed. "People of the city of the setting sun, look around! Beauty is everywhere and still you are not happy!"

The people shook their heads and muttered coarsely. "Happy! What do we have to be happy about?" they griped to one another.

"Let him try living in this mundane little town for a while," grumbled the mayor. "Let's see if he would still find beauty everywhere."

"Beauty, indeed! The man is mad!" cried a gray-haired woman. One by one, the people stood up and trudged back to their homes, concerned only with the weight of their worries.

The celestial visitor remained in the market square until all the people had left. The sky lost its blazing color and deepened to a crisp azure blue. A lone, bright star appeared and climbed above the horizon. "Ahh, the wishing star," whispered the stranger to himself. He stepped out of the market square and began to roam the crooked, cramped streets. It was a warm night and the voices of the townsfolk drifted out through the open windows. The complaints had softened into conversation. As the stranger listened, he became aware of the longing behind the grumbles.

"I made only three sales today," said a merchant to his wife. "This town has so few customers. I do not know how I will make ends meet and provide for all of us."

A young woman sat by the window and sewed. "Ouch," she cried as she pricked her finger with the needle. "How tired I am of sewing patches onto these old clothes. If only I had some cloth, I could make myself a new dress." Her husband sat nearby and when he did not answer, she mumbled under her breath. "Maybe then you would notice me."

A little boy whimpered for attention. "Papa, Papa, tell me a story." His father answered absentmindedly, "All I have is the same old stories. Aren't you tired of hearing them?"

"No Papa, I love them. Please tell them to me," begged the child.

A mild breeze stirred and gently carried every individual voice out into the night. Sighs mingled with moans, whimpers mixed with groans. The heavenly stranger took note of each one and carefully considered what he heard. One by one, the people blew out their candles and extinguished their lamps. Talking dissolved into silence as they climbed into their beds and fell sound asleep. The stranger continued walking through the quiet streets, the wants and wishes of the people slowly taking shape in his thoughts as the moon rose high into the charcoal sky, bathing the city and its slumbering inhabitants with a benevolent light. Finally, he arrived back at the market square. The light wind ruffled the waxy leaves of the magnificent tree, and they shimmered in the moonlight. The tree's generous branches stretched forth and beckoned to the angel. He smiled and floated up onto an overhanging bough. He leaned his back against the sturdy trunk, rested his slippered feet on the tree limb, reached into the pocket of his scarlet pants, and pulled out a silver flute.

The angel brought the flute to his lips and began to play. Like drops of rain falling onto the still surface of a pond, pure, distinct notes streamed out of the flute, blending into a delicate melody that rippled out of the tree and into the night air. The music floated in through the open windows, seeped into the ears of the sleeping townsfolk and lodged in their dreams. The rhythm grew more insistent, its throbbing pulse rousing the deepest worry harbored by each dreamer. The feelings of uneasiness grew stronger and stronger as the relentless beat continued, until each person could see the shape and feel the weight of their trouble. The angel blew one shrill penetrating note. Every one of them sat bolt upright in their beds, overcome by an urgent need to get up and leave their houses.

The people threw back their bedcovers, filed into the streets, and, in a frenzied wave, marched to the market square. They saw the angel standing beneath the tree, holding his silent flute in one hand.

"What is the meaning of all this?" shouted the mayor angrily.

The angel looked at the haggard, worn faces of the people before him with compassion. "The weight of your burdens has clouded your vision. Let go of your troubles and give them to me. Open your mouths and call forth your woes." He raised the flute to his lips once more and blew out a plaintive tune, beseeching the people to release their misery. A few people began to whimper softly, their sadness billowing into mournful howls. The remainder of the crowd quickly joined in. A collective wail arose from the people of such force that the lamentations became tangible. Stones and pebbles erupted from the mouths of the people and tumbled into a pile at the angel's feet. As every one of them spat out their trouble, the strength of their cry diminished until a hushed silence encompassed the entire assembly. Their bodies drooping with relief, the people stared incredulously at the jumbled heap of rubble that lay on the ground in front of the angel.

Tenderly, the angel addressed the crowd. "Here lie your worries, the burdens that have shaped your lives." He reached down and picked up a coal-black stone. Turning to the mayor, he spoke sympathetically: "This is the manifestation of your fear. You pace the floor at night, afraid that your efforts to help the people of this town will be inadequate. Look closely; let me show you the ache within that fear." The angel closed his hand around the coal and tightened his fist. When he opened his hand, in his palm lay a radiant diamond with a golden thread attached. "This," said the angel "is the shape of responsibility. This is your loving concern for the people you serve." The angel stretched his hand toward the tree and hung the diamond from the tip of a branch for all to see.

With patient deliberateness, the angel extracted rock after rock from the pile, naming the trouble and revealing the yearning hidden within. A husband's indifference took the form of a jagged piece of slate that surrounded a tender heart of topaz. The fire opal of creativity blazed underneath the granite of the accountant's austerity. A young mother's gritty impatience concealed the blue sapphire of devotion to her children. As each lump of stone became its jeweled essence, the angel reached up and carefully placed the glittering gem on a tree branch.

An old woman at the edge of the crowd pointed to a rough chunk of pumice. "That is mine," she croaked. "Please, show me my affliction." The angel retrieved the stone from the pile and beckoned the woman to come forward. "It is your loneliness," he said. "You pine away for your dead husband and the children who have moved away." He wrapped both of his hands around the stone and squeezed them together. Unclasping his grip, he revealed a dazzling ruby. "This is your wish to share your life with someone else."

Finally, there were no stones left in the pile. Instead, a dazzling rainbow of twinkling light radiated from the tree. The angel turned his face toward the tree and said, "Here are your troubles—the glimmering burdens that have shaped you. Look at the shining truth of who you are." The people gazed at the glittering tree and searched the branches for their particular jewel. As their eyes scanned the tree, they observed the wondrous variety and beauty of all the sparkling gems. A nagging wife found her husband's sparkling emerald. Lovingly, she reached over and clasped his hand. A young student, surprised by his teacher's pale amethyst, walked toward him and shyly thanked him for keeping order in the classroom. No longer consumed by their personal worries, the people discarded their isolation and offered each other apologies and compliments.

An atmosphere of thoughtfulness and consideration permeated the crowd. When the first hint of brightness crept into the night sky, the angel called out, "People, it has been a long and marvelous night. The time has come to sleep. Return to your homes and keep each other in your hearts." He put his flute to his lips, and the soothing notes of a lullaby floated out. The people turned to the angel and gratefully waved their thanks. They bid each other good-night and sleepily walked back home.

The mayor of that little town slept until the midmorning sunlight warmed his face, then eagerly climbed out of bed. He looked out the window and smiled an enthusiastic welcome to the new day. When he finished dressing, he sat down on the bed to put on his boots. He easily slipped on the right boot but when he put on the left, he felt an uncomfortable lump in the toe. Surprised, he reached inside, wriggled his fingers around until he clasped the troublesome object, and slowly pulled it out. He opened his fist and gasped when he saw what lay in his palm, his nocturnal diamond of responsibility. The mayor remembered the incredible happenings of the night before and, with a grateful heart, held the jewel up toward the window and watched it twinkle in the light.

Throughout the entire town, the same thing happened to each inhabitant. As every one of them put on their shoes, each discovered a lump in the toe and pulled out a jewel left by the angel, a glittering reminder of their true natures.

Our ordinary frustrations with daily life are often signals of a more profound discontent, a groaning that expresses a deeply felt longing. Examining these disappointments can offer rich insight into our lives as well as possibilities for change and growth. On the surface, our difficulties often masquerade as problems in need of solution. However, attentive exploration of our struggles can reveal hidden feelings, an emotional and spiritual landscape that shapes the core of our being. Seeing what is valuable in our experiences and learning to understand our feelings, even distressing ones of loneliness and sorrow, can help us live lives that are more meaningful. We learn to embrace who we are rather than wish for a life that is different from the one we have.

9

$\mathscr{P}eace\ \mathscr{T}hat\ \mathscr{L}asts$

A Buddhist Tale from India Retold

*O*nce, an argument erupted in the community of monks who resided at Kosambi. The quarrel grew so intense that the community split into two feuding sides who bickered back and forth, each group pointing the finger at the other. Unable to resolve their dispute, the monks descended upon the Buddha like a swarm of angry gnats and asked him to settle their differences.

"Be wary of causing divisions," the Buddha admonished them. "Do not cling to thoughts of past harm. Respect one another." However, the monks did not fully understand his teaching and they continued to disagree, reaching the point of violence. The people of Kosambi were disturbed by the monks' fierce discord and they withdrew their support from the monastery. When this happened, the monks returned to the Buddha and again asked his advice. The Buddha addressed the monks and told them this Story of the Past.

In former times, King Brahmadatta reigned over the great and prosperous Kingdom of Kasi. He resided in Benares in a splendid palace containing great treasures and commanded a mighty army. Nearby, Dighiti the Long-Suffering struggled to rule the tiny, poverty-stricken Kingdom of Kosala. However, Brahmadatta was not satisfied with his wealth and wanted more. Seeing the Kingdom of

Kosala, he thought to himself, "Dighiti's forces are weak and small. I can easily defeat his army and extend my boundaries." He called his generals together, assembled the army, and rode out to conquer Kosala.

Brahmadatta's army thundered across the land, the horses' hooves pounding against the ground. When Dighiti's watchmen felt the earth tremble beneath them, they looked out and saw Brahmadatta's powerful army with their swords raised, emerging from a cloud of dust. They ran to inform their king of the terrible sight. Dighiti realized that his puny forces could not resist Brahmadatta, and compassion filled his heart. He addressed his generals, "We cannot hope to win a battle against Brahmadatta. He will slaughter our people and destroy their homes. If we wish this kingdom to survive, we must surrender."

Then he turned to his wife and said, "We must leave this place. If Brahmadatta finds us, he will publicly humiliate and execute us. Let us go to Benares. It is a big city and Brahmadatta will not expect us to flee to our enemy's home. He will never look for us in his own city." Disguising themselves as wandering ascetics, they made their way to Benares, where they came upon an abandoned potter's hut. They settled on the outskirts of the city. Every day, Dighiti went out into the streets with his bowl and begged for alms to feed his wife and himself.

After a time, Dighiti's wife became pregnant. When the queen realized that she was with child, she became distressed. Turning to Dighiti, she moaned, "How can I bring a child into this world? Look at this squalid hut and those crowded, filthy streets. Our child deserves to be raised in a palace with all the privileges of royalty."

One day, a court priest arrived at Dighiti's cottage. When he saw the queen, he folded his hands in reverent salutation and prophesied, "Fear not, the king of Kosala is in your womb!" The prediction eased the queen's worries. She gave birth to a baby boy, whom they named Dighavu, the Long-Lived One.

One afternoon, as Dighiti watched his son playing happily in the street, anxiety overwhelmed him. He explained his apprehension to his wife. "People can forgive those who hurt them but they often harbor resentment toward those they hurt. King Brahmadatta has done us great harm and he fears our revenge. I worry about Dighavu's safety. If Brahmadatta discovers us, he will kill us—all three of us."

The queen pondered the matter for some time before she answered her husband. "I understand your concern. Let us send Dighavu to my relatives in the countryside. They will care for him and bring him up as a prince." With a deep sorrow that pierced their hearts, Dighiti and the queen sent Dighavu away to live with his mother's family, where he developed all the skills necessary to become a king.

Unfortunately, events unfolded just as Dighiti feared. King Brahmadatta's barber was from Kosala and had worked for Dighiti many years before. One afternoon, as the barber made his way through the busy marketplace, he spotted a familiar figure begging in the streets. Recognizing his former employer, the scheming barber saw an opportunity for his own advancement. He secretly followed Dighiti through the crowds and found out where he lived. Then he quickly returned to Brahmadatta's palace and, claiming he had important information, requested an audience with the king.

Brahmadatta listened intently as the barber explained his discovery and revealed the whereabouts of Dighiti and his wife. The king's hidden dread surfaced. Fearing that the royal couple were still plotting revenge, Brahmadatta turned to his soldiers and commanded them, "Take this man with you. He will lead you to Dighiti and his queen. Arrest them, bind their hands, shave their heads, and parade them through the streets to the edge of the city. Execute them and leave their bodies for the birds of the air to prey upon. I will be rid of these enemies once and for all!"

At the same time, young Dighavu was experiencing the pangs of longing. "I have not seen my parents for some time," he thought to himself. "How I miss my mother's sweet voice and my father's encouragement. I must go and see them." Dighavu left the countryside and made his way to the city. When he arrived, he spotted a commotion in the streets outside his parents' home and, sensing trouble, pushed his way through the crowd.

Dighiti looked up and saw Dighavu's face in the crowd. He did not want the army to detect his son's presence. Knowing that he was about to die, he also wanted to leave Dighavu with some advice that would guide him through the difficult times ahead. In a loud voice, he called out, "Dighavu, Dighavu. Be not shortsighted. Be not long-sighted. Hatred is not quenched by hatred; hatred is only appeased by love."

The crowd jeered at Dighiti. "The man is mad with fear," they cried. "He talks nonsense and gibberish."

However, Dighavu recognized his father's voice and he understood his warning. Silently, he ran along at the edge of the crowd, staring helplessly at his mother and father as the soldiers marched them through the streets. Dighiti saw his son's pained expression and, worried that he might try to intervene, called out again, "Dighavu, Dighavu! Be not shortsighted. Be not long-sighted. Hatred is not quenched by hatred; hatred is only appeased by love." Dighavu heard his father's words; he struggled to understand what they meant. He followed the soldiers out of the south gate of the city, where they forced his parents to kneel in the dirt.

Once more Dighiti called out, "Dighavu, Dighavu! Be not shortsighted. Be not long-sighted. Hatred is not quenched by hatred; hatred is only appeased by love." His father's dying words penetrated Dighavu's heart. He stared in mute horror as the soldiers executed his parents, chopping off their heads and tossing their bodies onto the street.

Dighavu could not leave his parents' bodies disrespectfully discarded. As the soldiers stood watch, he went into the city and bought some strong wine. When night fell, he returned to the city's edge and, walking up to the soldiers, said, "You have put in a hard day's work. You need something to relieve the strain of your labors," and he handed them each a bottle. The soldiers gladly accepted and soon lay drunk and sound asleep on the ground.

Dighavu collected pieces of wood and stacked them up. He dragged his parents' bodies out of the dirt, carefully placed them on top of the pile, and set the wood on fire. With palms pressed together, he walked around the funeral pyre three times, as the flames rose high into the night sky.

Brahmadatta had received word of Dighiti's execution. Restlessly, he paced his rooftop terrace, trying to grasp the meaning of Dighiti's final utterance. He looked out beyond the south gate and, in the very spot where the corpses had been thrown, saw the fire. As Brahmadatta watched the blaze, he became aware of the figure of a young man, reverently performing a funeral rite. "Surely this must be a kinsman of Dighiti's and he will seek revenge," he thought to himself. "Is there no end to this?" he cried, trying to shake the cold fear that clutched at his heart. "I need someone who can help me make sense of all of this," he whispered aloud.

When the funerary ritual was completed, Dighavu walked deep into the forest where he wept and wailed until all the tears had left his body. Numb and exhausted, he collapsed to the ground and slept for several days. When he awoke, the raw wound of his grief had hardened into resolve, and, in the dark recesses of his mind, a plan began to take shape. Dighavu went into the center of the city and found Brahmadatta's palace. He stood at the gates of the royal elephant barn and asked the elephant trainer, "How can I learn the art of training elephants?"

The master of the elephants looked Dighavu over and, judging him a capable young man, declared, "I will take you on as an apprentice and teach you how to train elephants." Dighavu learned quickly and his reliability and engaging manner endeared him to all who worked in the stables. Yet he kept his identity a secret, going by another name.

Dighavu often awakened early, before the light of day gilded the sky. It was his habit on those days to take his lute into the stable yard and play sweet melodies as he welcomed the dawn with a delicate song. One such morning Brahmadatta, whose dreams had not allowed him to sleep, restlessly prowled the palace grounds. When he reached an empty courtyard on the far side of the elephant barn, the sweet sound of Dighavu's music floated through the air and reached Brahmadatta's ears. As he listened, the burden of his troubling thoughts slowly eased and drifted away.

The music stopped and Brahmadatta returned to his bedchamber. Calling one of his servants, he asked, "This morning I heard a beautiful song that gladdened my heart. Who makes such music?"

His attendant replied, "The master of elephants has a young apprentice who is talented in many ways. I have heard that he likes to sing and play the lute. Perhaps it was him you heard."

"I would like to meet this young man," said Brahmadatta.

Later that morning, Dighavu appeared before the king. "Young man," said Brahmadatta, "was it you who played such a sweet melody this morning?"

"I was singing in the stable yard this morning," answered Dighavu.

"Sing for me now."

"As you wish, Your Majesty," and Dighavu sang a tantalizing song that charmed the king.

Brahmadatta was impressed with the young man's demeanor and abilities, and he said, "I could use someone of your sensibilities to wait on me."

"As you wish, Your Majesty," replied Dighavu, and he became Brahmadatta's personal attendant. Dighavu waited on the king; he always spoke politely and conducted himself in a pleasing manner. Dighavu's keen intelligence and responsiveness allowed him to gain a position of trust with the king.

One morning Brahmadatta summoned Dighavu and said, "Today I would like to go hunting. Gather my huntsmen together. Harness my chariot and bring it around."

"As you wish, Your Majesty," responded Dighavu, and he proceeded to organize the expedition. The hunting party gathered in the stable yard, and when Brahmadatta arrived, Dighavu gave him his weapons, escorted him to his chariot, and ceremoniously handed him the reins.

"You may drive my chariot today," said Brahmadatta.

"As you wish, Your Majesty." Dighavu led the men out of the gates of Benares, through the countryside, and into the forest beyond. As they raced through the tangled trees, Dighavu told the king, "Your Majesty, I am quite familiar with these woods. I know a better way."

"Very well," said Brahmadatta, and Dighavu drove the chariot away from the rest of the party, deep into the untamed woodlands.

After a time, Brahmadatta called out, "Stop, I am weary. Let us search for a place to rest." Dighavu found a secluded glade and unharnessed the horses from the chariot. Both men unbuckled their swords and sat down, side by side, underneath a banyan tree. "I am tired," said the king. He rested his head on Dighavu's lap and fell sound asleep.

Dighavu looked at the king asleep in his lap. He remembered his mother and father being marched through the city streets and his feelings of helplessness and rage. From the shadows of his mind, there arose a menacing thought. Slowly, he unsheathed his sword and held it above Brahmadatta's head. "Now, I could kill you. I could satisfy my anger and avenge my parents," he said to himself. As he held that sword above Brahmadatta's head, the dying words of Dighavu's father echoed in his ears and clarified his thoughts: "Be not shortsighted. Be not long-sighted. Hatred is not quenched by hatred; hatred is only appeased by love."

Dighavu lowered the sword and put it back in its sheath as tears streamed down his face. Again, the anguish and anger welled up inside Dighavu; he could almost smell the ashes of his parents' burnt bodies. He pulled the sword out of its casing and lifted it into the air. Amid the pain, he recalled his father's last hour and the plea that came from the depths of his soul: "Be not shortsighted. Be not long-sighted. Hatred is not quenched by hatred; hatred is only appeased by love." With trembling hands, he put the sword back in its scabbard.

As Dighavu sat there, another level of sorrow surfaced. He keenly felt the isolation of his childhood, the loneliness of living in exile away from his parents, a separation made necessary because of the loss of his father's kingdom. He took up the sword once more. Again, his father's words came back to him, words that were the only form of protection and legacy his father was able to offer. He could not dishonor his father by ignoring his guidance. He had to lay down his sword.

Brahamadatta awoke in a cold sweat.

"What is the matter, Your Majesty?" inquired Dighavu.

"I had a terrible dream, a dream that haunts me and that I cannot get rid of. In it, I learn that Dighiti, my enemy, had a son named Dighavu, who is coming after me with his sword raised trying to kill me and avenge the death of his parents."

Dighavu grabbed the king by his hair and yanked his head back onto the ground. With his right hand, he grabbed his sword and raised it. "I am Dighavu," he snarled, "and I will kill you and avenge my parents' death."

For a moment, Brahmadatta looked uncomprehendingly at the young man he had grown to trust—but then he saw the pain in Dighavu's eyes, heard the hatred in his voice, and felt the angry strength of his grip. "Please do not kill me," he begged. "Grant me my life."

Dighavu stared at him. "No, you foolish king, don't you understand? It is you who must grant me *my* life. For men can forgive those who hurt them, but they cannot forgive those they hurt. I will always be a reminder to you of your wrongdoing. You will see me as a threat to your peace of mind and your physical safety. You will seek to kill me so that you do not have to face me. No, my king, it is you who must grant me my life."

Fear eased its hold on Brahmadatta. "Grant me my life," he said to Dighavu, "and I will grant you yours."

Dighavu released his grip and set down his sword. The two men clasped hands and swore an oath never to harm one another.

"Let us go back to the palace," said Brahmadatta.

"As you wish, Your Majesty," replied Dighavu.

When they arrived back at the palace, Brahmadatta called together his councillors. With Dighavu at his side, he addressed them and asked, "If you saw Dighavu, son of my enemy Dighiti, what would you do?"

The councillors raucously shouted their affirmations of loyalty. "Cut off his hands! Cut off his feet! Chop off his head!"

Then Brahmadatta spoke. "Listen to me," he said, lifting his open palm toward Dighavu, "this is Prince Dighavu." The astonished councillors immediately grabbed the hilts of their swords. "No harm must come to him," commanded Brahmadatta. "He has granted me my life and I have granted him his."

Turning to Dighavu, he said, "Your father's dying words have pre-occupied my thoughts on many sleepless nights. Can you help me understand them? What did he mean when he said, 'Be not short-sighted'?"

Dighavu answered, "The words mean, cherish friendship. Do not be quick to fall out with friends."

"What did he mean when he said, 'Be not long-sighted'?"

"He meant, do not dwell on thoughts of past harm, for then hatred will endure," said Dighavu

"What did he mean when he said, 'Hatred is not quenched by hatred; hatred is only appeased by love'?"

"Your Majesty," explained Dighavu, "you stole my father's king-dom and murdered my parents. If I avenged their death and killed you, then your kinsmen would kill me. In turn, my relatives would kill them. There would be no end to the hatred and bloodshed. But now, I have granted you your life and you have granted me mine. We can live together in peace."

Brahmadatta stood before his council and said, "How remarkable it is for this young man to understand the depth of these short sen-tences. Listen to him, for he is wise indeed." Brahmadatta restored the Kingdom of Kosala to Prince Dighavu, its rightful heir and ruler. In time, Prince Dighavu married Brahmadatta's daughter and the two kingdoms existed, side by side, in peace and harmony.

With this story, the Buddha helped the monks achieve awareness of their harmful thoughts. They welcomed his words and learned to live together peaceably.

"Do not cling to thoughts of past harm. Respect one another." Buddha's teaching to the monks reflects great wisdom. There are times when a particular

memory exerts such a profound effect on us that it shapes our perception of who we are and determines how we relate to various people in our life. A memory can become so deeply rooted that we are no longer aware of its influence on our thinking. Memories attached to feelings of anger or hatred bind us to the past and trap us in patterns of destructive behavior. Individuals remain in conflict because certain issues are never resolved. We remember the pain and perpetuate the blame.

Changing our entrenched attitudes is a difficult, slow process. We need to become cognizant of memory's hold on us. A specific event may trigger this awareness, or an insightful person or spiritual teacher may prompt us to reconsider our way of thinking. As we examine our previous experiences, we must learn to retell the story of our life. We accept that there is another side to the story and actively choose new ways of looking at the past. In this way, we reconcile ourselves to the past and are able to forgive those who have hurt us. We are able to continue our journey unburdened.

10

The Rich Man and the Shoemaker

A European Jewish Tale Retold

Daylight darkened into evening and a brisk winter wind gusted through the narrow streets of a tiny, crowded city, rattling the windowpanes and threatening to blow the hats off the heads of those making their way home after a long day's work. A weary traveler trudged along, searching for a hint of welcome in the drab houses that lined the winding avenues of the Jewish quarter of the city. His pockets were empty, he had not eaten all day, and as he wrapped his tattered coat more tightly around his frail body, he began to shiver from the cold. He turned the corner and saw a lone house across the square, its sturdy brick exterior protecting it from the blustery weather. Inviting, amber light emanated from the velvet-curtained windows and spilled out onto the street below. The traveler hurried across the square and rapped his ungloved fist against the heavy wooden door. No one answered. He knocked more insistently. An unseen hand shut the velvet curtains, extinguishing the light and any hope of hospitality.

In desperation, the traveler called out, "Please, let me in. I am cold and hungry. Surely, someone as rich as you can spare a coin or two to help a poor man." The door remained closed. Dejected, he started to walk away and almost bumped into a man hurrying down the street.

"Don't waste your time there," said the man. "He never parts with his money. He lives there all alone, without a care for anyone but himself. If you are in need, my friend, I suggest you go to the shoemaker's house. He never turns anyone away." He pointed straight ahead and gave the traveler directions. "It's the seventh house on your right. You can't miss it. It's the one with the bright blue door."

"Thank you," said the traveler. With the wind at his back, he headed off, carefully counting houses as he walked down the street. When he came to the seventh house, he knocked on the blue door. A man in a leather apron opened it, and before the traveler could explain his predicament, the shoemaker greeted him and motioned for him to enter the house.

"Come on in. It's a terrible night to be outside." The traveler stepped inside, stammered his thanks, and gave a timid bow. A pot of soup bubbled in the fireplace, filling the small room with a delicious fragrance. Without thinking, the traveler lifted his face, breathed in deeply, and exhaled with a soulful sigh.

"You must be hungry. Sit down and have a bowl of soup," said the shoemaker, gesturing toward the long table where his family was sitting. The traveler settled himself on a rustic bench next to the cobbler's rosy-cheeked children whose smiling faces indicated they were accustomed to sharing their supper with strangers. The shoemaker's wife ladled soup into bowls and placed the first one in front of the traveler. His eyes widened as he saw the thick chunks of cabbage, onion, and potato swimming in the rich broth, and he picked up his spoon in eager anticipation. The shoemaker took off his leather apron and sat down. He reverently bent his head over his bowl, acknowledging his thankfulness for the blessings of good food and family in an earnest voice. The traveler impatiently nodded his assent and quickly gulped down his soup in noisy slurps. When he finished, the cobbler's wife, without hesitation, gave him another bowlful, as well as several slices of dark, dense bread.

The second bowl of soup awakened the traveler's sense of propriety. Turning to the cobbler's wife, he said, "Thank you for your kindness. I haven't had a bowl of soup this good in years. Your husband is a lucky man!" The traveler and the shoemaker began to swap stories. The shoemaker's children chimed in, embellishing his tales with assorted details until that tiny room was filled with laughter. The children cleared the dishes away and the cobbler's wife served a rich sweet cake made with raisins and nuts. As the traveler ate his dessert, he glanced about the room. The sparse accommodations stood in marked contrast to the plentiful meal. A few wooden shelves held minimal cooking utensils and supplies. A few feet away from the rustic table and benches, a lone rocking chair occupied the corner of the room and a three-legged stool sat next to the fireplace. The remainder of the room was devoted to the cobbler's workshop, a simple bench that held a rudimentary assortment of tools and a pile of leather.

That night, the traveler slept on the floor next to the fireplace, on a makeshift bed of old quilts and blankets. In the morning, he thanked the cobbler and his wife for their generous hospitality. As the traveler prepared to leave, the shoemaker lifted the lid from a jar on his workbench and handed him two silver coins. "To ease your journey," he said with a smile.

In the spring, word went through the town that the rich man had died. No one mourned his passing. "Stingy old fellow," muttered some of the townsfolk. "He never cared for anyone but himself."

"Yes," mumbled others, "he just stayed locked up in that fine big house. Who will miss him?" Only the rabbi and the undertaker followed the funeral procession to the cemetery. They buried the rich man near the fence, in a place reserved for beggars and outcasts.

The townspeople continued to ask the shoemaker for help in times of need. However, after a few weeks, he no longer invited folks in for supper and began to turn people away, saying, "I'm sorry. I cannot help you." The rabbi was puzzled by the shoemaker's change of heart and went to see him. "Come in, Rabbi," said the cobbler with a reluctant sigh and slowly opened the blue door. "Can I offer you a cup of tea?"

Accustomed to a slice of cake or a piece of kugel, the rabbi expressed surprise at the meager offering. "Tea?" he asked in surprise. "Is that all you can offer?"

"Yes, Rabbi," said the shoemaker. "Things are not what they once were."

"I don't understand," said the rabbi. "People count on you to help them out. What has happened to your generosity?"

"Ah, Rabbi," said the cobbler. "It breaks my heart to turn people away. Look around," said the shoemaker, gesturing toward his shelves. "I barely have enough to feed my family. Making shoes is a difficult way to earn a living. I was only able to help people because of the rich man."

"What do you mean?" asked the rabbi.

The shoemaker answered, "It is a long story. The rich man used to disguise himself and walk through the streets of the city. When he saw people in need, he came to me with money and instructions. It was because of him that I was able to offer food to the bricklayer's widow. When the baker's shop caught fire, the rich man appeared at my back door that night with money for lumber and supplies. Every household on this street has benefited from his kindness," remarked the cobbler.

The rabbi puzzled over the unexpected information that the shoemaker had just shared. "Why didn't he give the money to the people himself?"

"He was afraid they would thank him and praise him," explained the cobbler.

"That makes no sense," said the rabbi.

"He wanted to give out of compassion. If people knew of his good deeds, they would thank him and he might begin to offer charity so that he could receive praise. He did not want to be tempted by pride, so he remained anonymous. Unfortunately, now that he is dead, there is no more money! I am so sorry that I can no longer help people."

"You are a good man," said the rabbi, placing his hand on the cobbler's shoulder in commonplace benediction.

As the rabbi walked home, he observed the traces of the rich man's hidden benevolence. The bricklayer's son ran out into the street to retrieve a ball, his well-fed face smiling at the rabbi. People happily filed out of the bakery with loaves of bread and boxes of pastry. That evening, the rabbi called the townsfolk together and told them the truth about the rich man. Touched by the astounding news, the people assembled at the rich man's grave to pay their respects. Every day the rabbi visited the gravesite to honor the rich man's memory. When he died, the rabbi left instructions that he was to be buried near the fence beside the rich man.

Our gifts to others often carry with them the expectation of something in return. We like to see our name included on the donor list, we bask in public acknowledgment of our volunteer efforts, and we wait expectantly for thank-you notes for graduation gifts and wedding presents. We attach a certain importance to the outcome of our efforts, hoping that others will reinforce our good opinion of ourselves and give us the credit we think we deserve. Authentic generosity is unconditional. Out of love for others and recognition of their needs, we offer our money, our time, and our hospitality with no strings attached.

However, giving is only half the equation. In this story, the rich man remains anonymous because he does not want his giving to become tinged with pride. While a benevolent attitude urges us to share what we possess, it also can make us aware of the abilities and talents of others. Oftentimes, it is more difficult to receive than to give, but it is important to accept the offerings of those around us. As we participate in this exchange of support for one another, we come to understand that everybody can give and we all have some aspect of our life to share with others.

11

The Spirit of
the Rice Fields

An Indonesian Myth Retold

Long, long ago, hidden deep within the clouds and mist beyond the highest mountaintops of Java, there was a palace of light and air where Batara Guru, the father of all the gods, lived with his sons and his radiantly beautiful daughter Tisna Wati. Batara Guru ruled the kingdom of the heavens and upheld the balance of the universe. Whenever the forces of chaos threatened to disrupt the cosmos, Batara Guru and his sons would descend to earth to battle their enemies and maintain order. Tisna Wati never joined them; she remained safe and protected within the solid rainbow walls of the palace.

Batara Guru sequestered himself and his sons within his chambers whenever it was necessary to prepare for combat. The walls of light surrounding his rooms glowed red with the intensity of their deliberations and the air became charged with anticipation. One day, Tisna Wati lingered outside her father's rooms, feeling the heat of the power within and longing to be part of the excitement. Her father emerged wearing full battle regalia, his features hardened into sharp severity by the weight of his responsibility. "Please, Father," Tisna Wati pleaded. "Let me come with you."

Batara Guru gazed at the innocent face of his daughter. Her love-liness brought a smile to his lips. He raised his broad hand and gently cupped her chin. "No, my beautiful child, stay here out of harm's way. There is no need for you to become involved with the rough matters of the world below," he said in a grave voice.

Tisna Wati paced from room to room, trying to ease her restless-ness. Unable to bear the hollow sound of her footsteps as they echoed through the empty corridors, she decided to escape the confines of the palace and explore the heavens. She stepped out into the mist, and the gentle wind began to blow. Tisna Wati felt it swirl around her ankles and flutter through her hair. Delighted by the warm air, she lifted her face toward the soft breeze and raised her arms, twirling round and round as it floated over her body. The gusts became stronger, parting the fog, uncovering a pathway, and propelling Tisna Wati through the haze. Laughing, she raced along until she came to a place where the veils of vapor thinned. Through the wisps, she caught glimpses of green and blue. Spurred on by her curiosity, she searched for an opening and soon discovered a break in the ragged clouds.

Tisna Wati peered through the gap and saw a vibrant world of dazzling beauty sprawled below her. Knobby green mountains nes-tled against one another like rows of mossy knuckles hunched over the earth. Tucked into their folds were forests of palm trees, their tufts of gray-green leaves perched atop long, slender trunks. Rice fields blanketed the land in a vivid patchwork of terraced strips of lush emerald plants climbing up hillsides, patches of brown seedlings sprouting from waterlogged paddies, and ditches of blue water sparkling in the sunlight.

Throughout this stunning terrain, men, women, and children worked side by side, their lively chatter buzzing through the fields. Tisna Wati watched the sweat pour off the wiry backs of the farmers as they plowed the fields. She stared at the women, backs hunched over as they plunged rice seedlings into the soil. Many of them car-ried babies in slings. When the infants began to cry, the women straightened up and nursed their children, standing ankle-deep in the mud. Children ran along pathways, laughing and chasing each other as their parents reprimanded them and urged them to get back to work. When noontime came, families left the fields and clustered together to share a meal. A wife wiped the sweat from her husband's forehead; a mother absentmindedly fed morsels of food to her two children as she chatted with a neighbor; a father stroked the cheek of his infant son. Everywhere Tisna Wati looked, she saw people connected to one another, their lives entwined in a common purpose forged from necessity coupled with tenderness. She could not take her eyes off them.

When the bright light of day softened, the people ceased their labor, retreated to their huts, and a hush came over the land. A lone star appeared in the azure sky. As it made its entrance, a single clear note sounded and hung in the air. Tisna Wati scanned the landscape looking for the source of this sound and saw a handsome young rice farmer, sitting cross-legged at the edge of his rice field, holding a bamboo flute to his lips. One note deliberately followed another, dancing into a delicate melody that drifted up to the heavens and greeted the stars as they twinkled into the night. It was the most beautiful music that Tisna Wati had ever heard.

Day after day, Tisna Wati made her way to the break in the clouds and stared downward, feeling the throb and pulse of the world below. She became familiar with individual faces and recognized the daily routine of each one. She watched an old woman trudge home alone each afternoon, and wanted to walk beside her simply to ease the burden of her loneliness. She delightfully observed the playful antics of a group of children as they splashed each other with water from the fields and shook her head when their stern father rebuked them with harsh words. Tisna Wati surveyed the activities of all the people but her gaze never strayed too far from the handsome young rice farmer. She eagerly awaited nightfall so that she could hear him play his bamboo flute. As she listened to his exquisite music, Tisna Wati's heart awakened and she fell in love.

Whenever Batara Guru returned from combat, he summoned Tisna Wati to his chambers. Battling chaos left him weary and ragged, and he looked forward to the reassuring presence of his lovely daughter. This time, however, Tisna Wati seemed preoccupied. Batara Guru was surprised by her behavior: She didn't pester him for details about the campaign against his enemies, and her answers to his questions were short and monotonous. He examined the dreamy look on her face and surmised the difficulty. "Tisna Wati," he sighed, "I think it is time for me to find you a husband!"

At the mention of the word *husband*, Tisna Wati's wistful expression vanished. She looked directly at her father and said, "There's no need for you to do that. I have found one already."

Batara Guru raised his eyebrows and cast a questioning glance toward his daughter. "What do you know about choosing a husband?" he asked, irritation edging his voice. "I am your father and I understand these things. I will find you a proper husband."

"Please, Father," begged Tisna Wati, "just come with me and see." Batara Guru followed his daughter out of the palace and through the mist. He saw the lightness in her feet and her flushed face. With every step they took, his heart stiffened in apprehension. They came to the opening in the clouds. "There he is," said Tisna Wati and with a trembling hand pointed her finger, directing her father's eye toward her beloved rice farmer.

Batara Guru stared at the young man, knee-deep in water, back bent as he toiled in his rice field. "You want to marry a man of the earth? No, Tisna Wati, such a thing is impossible. You are immortal … you have drunk the life water … you cannot marry a human being." Batara Guru's impatience flared into anger. "No, I forbid it. I will find you a proper husband."

Tisna Wati saw her father's face contorted in rage and she knew better than to argue with him. She pressed her lips together and followed him off to the side all the way home.

It was not long before turmoil once again threatened to upset the stability of the universe. Batara Guru marshaled his sons; they made the necessary preparations and donned their battle gear. Before he left, Batara Guru summoned his daughter to bid her good-bye. Tisna Wati perfunctorily kissed her father on the cheek but did not reach out to embrace him. Her unresponsiveness caused him to hesitate. He brushed her cheek with his rugged fingers, then turned and, with a heavy heart, left the palace.

As soon as they were gone, Tisna Wati ran out into the clouds and called to the wind, "Please come. I need your help." A faint breeze stirred and when Tisna Wati felt the warm air on her skin, she implored the wind, "Please, I must see the rice farmer. Take me down to him. Take me down to the earth." Tisna Wati watched as the clouds began to shiver and tremble. Slowly, they coalesced into tiny feathers that danced into formation and became two delicate ivory wings fluttering before her. She climbed into the sheltering pocket between the wings and knelt down as the wind carried her through the clouds, out of the mist, and into the bright blue sky. The wings floated through the sky, drifting closer and closer to the earth, allowing Tisna Wati to feel the denseness of the air and breathe in its pungent aroma.

The wings hovered silently over the ground, deposited Tisna Wati near the rice field, then flapped once and evaporated. The softness of her landing made no sound, but as her feet touched the sun-warmed soil, she let out a delighted gasp. The farmer turned and watched in wonder as Tisna Wati gracefully glided toward him. She was the most beautiful woman he had ever seen. Tisna Wati stood before him and spoke. "I am Tisna Wati. I have come from the heavens above." Her voice sounded like birdsong greeting the dawn and the rice farmer was overwhelmed with love.

"Why are you here?" he asked.

"I have come looking for a husband," said Tisna Wati. Unbridled joy burst forth from the farmer as he threw back his head and let loose a peal of laughter. Tisna Wati joined him, giggling with deep pleasure. The music of their merriment reverberated across the fields and resounded through the hollow sky.

The sound of their uncontained joy penetrated the battlefield amid the clashing and clanging of swords. Batara Guru recognized Tisna Wati's tinkling laugh. The sound of it triggered such alarm within him that he dropped his sword immediately and fled to the rice field. He found Tisna Wati with the young farmer. Enraged by her impudence, he roared, "How dare you! Return to the heavens at once! Go back where you belong!"

Tisna Wati faced her father and hurled her words toward him. "No, I will not go back to the empty heavens. I want to stay here. This is where I belong."

Batara Guru looked at his daughter standing defiantly before him, at the edge of a common rice field, mud seeping between the toes of her tiny feet. "Then stay you shall!" he bellowed out in a voice that shook the hills. He raised his mighty arm and extended his palm toward Tisna Wati. Minute sparks of blue-white lightning crackled and flashed, igniting the air with sizzling light. Unable to bear the brightness, the rice farmer bent his head, closed his eyes, and covered them with his hands. After a moment, Batara Guru pulled back his arm and clenched his fist, and the sparks fizzled out.

The rice farmer quickly opened his eyes, searching for Tisna Wati, but her body was gone. In her place was a delicate rice plant with elegant, tapered green leaves. Batara Guru looked at the slender stalk and said, "Tisna Wati, now you are a daughter of the earth. Your spirit is one with this rice field. Here you will live forever!" Reluctantly, he turned away and went back to the heavens.

A light breeze stirred, and the rice plant bent toward the young farmer as if trying to embrace him. He knelt and tenderly stroked the plant with loving fingers. Then he sat next to the plant, took out his flute, and began to play. He played until the colors of the day faded and the earth was wrapped in darkness. He continued into the morning of the next day and the day after that. So great was his sorrow that he could not stop, and his mournful music ascended into the sky and pierced the heavens. Batara Guru listened and his heart was touched by the faithfulness of the young man.

He found the ragged tear in the clouds and stood looking down at the graceful rice plant and the young farmer. Batara Guru knew that a god's action was his word; it was final. He could not change what he had done. Tisna Wati's soul was in the rice plant. Batara Guru raised his hand once more and sent forth an effervescent shower of glittering sparks. They fell to the earth and surrounded the rice farmer. When the sparks cleared, the young man had been transformed into a rice plant.

The two plants stood side by side, bent lovingly toward each other. The wind came and rippled over the land, caressing the rice fields with its tender touch. Batara Guru gazed at the two rice plants as they swayed and danced together, the ache in his heart softened by their willowy beauty.

In Southeast Asia, rice is celebrated as a sacred grain. Many rituals for cultivation and harvesting reflect the belief that each grain of rice contains the spirit of the Divine. In Indonesia, the guardian of the crops is the Rice Mother, a goddess whose body produced the first rice. Without proper respect, the soul of the rice will depart and the grains will no longer nourish the people or grow in the soil.

Boundaries establish order in our world, allowing us to define what is sacred and profane, what is acceptable and what is not. Boundaries can also hem us in and restrict growth. There are times when it becomes necessary to break through conventional boundaries to bring forth new ideas and make necessary changes. Ancient myths contain many gods and heroes who transgress the borders of heaven to bring new discoveries and gifts to the world of humans. A Greek myth describes how Prometheus scooped up mud and created human beings. These new creatures stood upright and gazed heavenward, but seemed frail and weak in comparison to the animals that possessed wings, fins, scales, and claws. In defiance of Zeus's prohibition, Prometheus stole fire from the divine flame on Mount Olympus and gave it to humans, enabling them to survive on the earth. Zeus was enraged and sent forth his minions, Force and Violence, who chained Prometheus to a rocky ledge on Mount Caucasus, where he was condemned to stay for all time while an eagle gnawed away at his innards.

Societies develop rules and codes of conduct that allow people to function within the group. However, in times of instability or change, the old norms are challenged because they no longer seem to work. A hero emerges who seeks a higher truth, envisions a new way of doing things, and makes a conscious sacrifice to integrate this idea into a new social fabric. This journey is never easy; the hero and his or her followers face turmoil, resistance, even death. During a time of great unrest in our own country, Dr. Martin Luther King Jr. confronted a prevailing system of injustice. His dream of equality ignited the civil rights movement and spurred the beginning of a cultural transformation.

As individuals, we often reach a point of personal crisis or experience a void in our lives. Our customary patterns of behavior cannot solve these problems. Oftentimes, our old habits have contributed to our difficulties. We need to find new ways of seeing the world and understanding ourselves. This search can be very painful and involves peeling away false perceptions and restructuring prescribed roles. If we do not risk this quest, we remain stagnant, unable to escape the constraints that keep us from becoming our true selves.

12

The Squire's Party

A Sufi Tale Retold

*E*very year the squire threw a big party for all the people in his little village in the Irish countryside to prove his magnanimity and reinforce his good opinion of himself. Even the tenants on his farms were invited to join in the festivities. When the day of the gala arrived, the squire sent his servants through the village and into the fields to remind everyone to come and join in the night's revelry. Late in the day, the servants arrived at Patrick Reilly's place and they found him digging up potatoes from his field. "Patrick," they shouted, "have you forgotten about the squire's party? Get out of the field and get ready."

Patrick put down his hoe and went inside to wash up. He scrubbed the dirt from underneath his fingernails as best he could, combed his hair, and kicked the soil from his brogans. Then he started the long walk down the lane toward the squire's fine house. When he arrived at the front door, the party was in full swing. The servants took one look at Patrick's coarse attire and exclaimed, "Patrick, you can't come in here dressed like that!"

"What do you mean?" asked Patrick.

"Look at your clothes—they've still got the dirt of the field on them," said the servants.

"Oh," said Patrick, looking down at his everyday pants. He turned around and made the long walk back home. Patrick took out the only other clothes he possessed—a suit that he wore to weddings, funerals, and the fair; a white shirt; and a red tie. He took out his good black boots, put them on, and returned to the squire's house just as the first star appeared in the night sky. This time when the servants saw Patrick all dressed up, they opened up the front door and ushered him in.

Inside the great room, Patrick saw a crowd of people eating, drinking, and having a good time. Fine linen covered the tables, and the good china sparkled in the light from the silver candelabras. The squire stood off to one side, observing the crowd with a great deal of satisfaction. Patrick made his way over to the main table, piled high with roasts, savory meat pies, and an assortment of breads and cheeses. He selected his food without bothering to use a plate. He took two thick slices of roast beef and jammed them into the pockets of his trousers. He grabbed several currant buns, stuffing a couple up each shirtsleeve and putting the remaining ones in his shirt pocket. He took a piece of pie and crammed it into the front pocket of his suit coat. The squire watched Patrick's peculiar antics and the wide smile on his face shrank to a frown.

No one else seemed to notice Patrick until he went over to the table where the spirits were kept. He took off his leather boot, held it up in the air, and poured whiskey into it until it was filled to the brim. People shook their heads and began to whisper to one another. The squire's mouth opened wide and the color drained from his cheeks. The fiddler and his band began to play, and everyone started to dance. Patrick took off his suit jacket and in a loud voice inquired, "May I have this dance?" The assembly broke into peals of laughter as they watched Patrick weave his way across the floor, twirling his jacket about and dancing with great delight.

The squire could keep quiet no longer and in a fury rushed over to Patrick and bellowed, "Patrick Reilly, what is the meaning of all this?" The crowd stopped their giggling and waited for Patrick's answer.

"Well, sir, it's like this," explained Patrick, draping his jacket over his arm. "When I first came to your house this evening, I was dressed in my ordinary clothes. Your servants turned me away. They said I wasn't dressed properly. So, I went home and changed my clothes. When I came back, they saw my good suit and let me in. Since I was the same person both times, I could only conclude that it wasn't me you were interested in having at the party, just my clothes. And so I am trying to fulfill your intentions and make sure that my clothes have the time of their lives."

This tale is based on a story of the Mulla Nasrudin or Joha, a wise fool who appears in Islamic and Arabic literature as well as in the folklore of Greece, Italy, Russia, France, China, and Pakistan. The Sufis use the stories of Nasrudin as spiritual teaching exercises, claiming that if people take in one of these tales and ponder it, allowing it to become part of them, the story can lead to higher wisdom.

Fools make us laugh and shake us free from our preoccupation with ourselves and our daily affairs. Their outrageous antics and unlikely observations turn the world upside down and reveal our limited understanding. For a moment, we can peek through the crack in the order of things and see our folly. They prick the skin of our self-importance and free us from the stranglehold of useless habits, all leading to a deeper appreciation of life and spirit.

13

Daniel's Legacy

A Liberian Folktale Retold

aniel stood on the porch in the early morning dimness, staring out at the darkened farm. In his mind's eye, he could see lush fields of corn and grain, rich green pastures filled with healthy cows grazing. As the sky brightened, the clear blue ribbon edging the horizon revealed the actual situation—stunted crops unable to grow because of lack of rain, a few skinny cows nibbling on tufts of grass in a dusty meadow. These were hungry times. Poor crops and fewer cattle meant less money, and he had not earned enough to make the annual payment for the farm. Daniel had worked hard for many years and could not bear the thought of losing his home. After much deliberation, he decided to travel to the city to find work, so he could come up with the necessary cash. When the rooster crowed his customary greeting to the dawn, a wry smile crept across Daniel's lips. Never before had he loved this place as much as he did today, the day of his departure.

Daniel walked into the kitchen where Lila was bustling about making breakfast, putting a pot of coffee on the stove, and cracking eggs into a thick, blue bowl. She looked at her husband's somber face and reassured him, "It'll be all right, Daniel. I can take care of the farm. The boys are getting older and they'll be a big help. You just go and do what you've got to do." Soon the two boys joined Daniel and Lila in the kitchen. They all sat together at the big table, eating their breakfast in silence, no one able to find the right words.

After breakfast, Daniel went upstairs. He placed his toilet articles next to the clean clothes Lila had packed in the rectangular suitcase with the wooden handle. He looked around their bedroom for an object to bring with him, something tangible to remind him of where he belonged in the world. He reached into his top bureau drawer and pulled out the gold pocketwatch his father had given him. He tied one end of a piece of twine around the stem, anchored the other to his belt loop, and put the watch in his pocket. Then he shut the suitcase and went downstairs.

Long good-byes didn't suit Daniel or his family; they just stretched out the inevitable and gave voice to the sadness. Daniel looked at his younger son, who was nicknamed Tad because he was so tiny, and ruffled his hair. "Make sure you help your mother," he cautioned. He turned to his older son, Simon, shook his hand and calmly remarked, "You're the man of the house now. Keep an eye on things!" He kissed Lila and summed up his love and dedication in three words: "I'll be back." He turned around, stepped off the porch, and headed out toward the county highway to catch the bus into the city.

Lila and her sons watched his broad shoulders and strong back until he reached the gate that opened into the lane, then Lila said, "Okay, boys, it's time to start our day. There's work to be done."

The owner of the general store in town had given Daniel the name of a friend to contact in the city. When Daniel arrived, he asked directions at the bus station and made his way through the maze of streets. The wide avenues with their tall buildings crowded next to each other seemed familiar to Daniel. As a high school student, he had accompanied his uncle, a salesman, into the boroughs on several occasions. However, the hum and thrum of city life made him uneasy. Amid the noise and frenzied commotion, he could never find a still place that made him feel protected, a place where he felt safe enough to rest.

When he reached his destination, Daniel introduced himself to Mr. Faraday and explained his situation. Mr. Faraday welcomed him, gave him the name of a decent boardinghouse, and said, "Work isn't easy to find these days. Your best bet is to show up early in the morning at the corner of Sixth Street and Kinsey Avenue. There's a fellow there who always needs day laborers for construction work." Daniel thanked him for his help. As he walked toward the boardinghouse, he tried to keep a firm grasp on his hopes; he put his hand in his pocket and rubbed his fingers across the smooth, hard surface of his gold pocketwatch.

Mrs. Johnson, a no-nonsense woman, ran the boardinghouse. She provided breakfast and supper, clean sheets, and a congenial atmosphere for a modest weekly fee. Daniel paid the money in advance and sat down for his evening meal with a group of strangers, men like himself, trying to earn enough to send money back home to their families. Being a day laborer was uncertain work; some days you were picked to join the construction crew and some days you weren't. By the end of the first week, he had earned enough to pay Mrs. Johnson but nothing more. Nevertheless, he wrote Lila a promising letter, explaining that he was sure things would get better. Two more weeks passed and things did not improve. Daniel often paced the floor at night, trying to ease his worries as he stroked the shiny cover of his gold pocketwatch.

One evening, a newcomer to Mrs. Johnson's house approached Daniel with a proposition. "Listen, I hear you're looking to make some money. I work for a company that repossesses cars. We could use a big, strong fellow like you. The work isn't easy but the pay is good. What do you say?"

Daniel hesitated; the idea of taking back someone's automobile sounded disagreeable, but he was growing desperate. Finally, he nodded his head. "All right, I'll give it a try."

The first car that Daniel and his partner repossessed belonged to a man who had a wife and three children. When Daniel showed him the section of the loan papers that allowed them to reclaim the car if the payments weren't made on time, the man begged for another chance. He swore that his luck would change. As they drove away, Daniel's coworker turned to him and said, "They all say that. Luck's a funny thing. It can go from good to bad at the drop of a hat!" That night, Daniel couldn't find much to say during supper. All he could think of was the look on the man's face as they drove away in his car, a look of humiliation and defeat.

In one week's time, Daniel made more money than he had during his entire stint as a day laborer. He was able to pay Mrs. Johnson her weekly rent, put some money in the bank, and still have a little left over to send to Lila. Despite the harshness of his duties, he continued his employment. He tried not to listen to people's excuses, but their pleas wormed their way into his thoughts. At night, he dreamed that the bank foreclosed on his farm, and Lila and his boys were left to wander the world alone. His nightmares made him keep his job; he had to earn enough money to make sure that his farm was never taken away.

Early one morning, Daniel and his partner took a bus to the outskirts of the city. They walked through streets lined with plain brick houses until they found the correct address. A wiry little man met them on the front stoop. When Daniel tried to explain that the loan gave them certain legal rights, the man shouted, "You're not going to take my car," picked up a baseball bat, and swung it at Daniel's head. Daniel ducked but his partner became so infuriated that he yanked the bat from the man's hands and threw it into the street.

"You miserable little fool," he hollered as he grabbed hold of the front of the man's shirt and slammed him against the doorframe. Daniel tried to stop his partner, but years of frustration poured out of the man's fists. He pummeled the other man until he lay crumpled on his front step, his body bruised and unmoving.

Later that day, the police arrested Daniel and his partner and put them in jail. The court appointed a public defender to represent Daniel, but the lawyer was young and inexperienced. Despite a plea for mercy, Daniel was sentenced to four years in prison.

Daniel could not figure out how to set things right. He agonized over what to say to Lila and spent two days writing her a letter explaining what had happened. He gave the letter to his lawyer and asked him to mail it to his wife, along with his gold pocketwatch and his other belongings. The lawyer gathered Daniel's things in a paper bag and took them to his office. When he got around to packing them into a box, the letter inadvertently fell to the floor. He never noticed it, and sent the package to Lila without an explanation.

Lila took the parcel from the postman's hands and examined it. The handwriting was unfamiliar and there was no return address; the only information about the sender was a city postmark. She sliced open the tape with a knife, slowly began to extract her husband's rumpled shirts, dirty socks, and soiled trousers from the box, and dropped them into a heap on the kitchen floor. Lila emptied his pockets one by one, searching for some small clue that would help her decipher the meaning behind this disheveled mound of clothes. All she found were tiny scraps of paper covered with Daniel's writing, big block letters scratched out quickly in pencil. There were street addresses next to the make and model numbers of cars. None of it made any sense to Lila. At the bottom of the box lay Daniel's gold pocketwatch. She picked it up and held it in her hand, tears starting to well up in her eyes. The watch was Daniel's most treasured possession; he would never give it up, not without a good reason.

Lila took out the letters he had written to her and read them over again, hoping to find the name of someone she could contact. Daniel was never very good with details; the notes talked about the noise of the city, his plans for the future, how much he missed her and the boys, but he did not mention the names of any friends or acquaintances, nor did he tell her the name of the place where he was staying. Her letters to him simply bore his name and a street address. Lila sat down at the kitchen table, pen in hand, and began scribbling notes starting with "To Whom It May Concern," inquiring about Daniel's whereabouts. Lila wrote a letter for every address she found in his pocket, stacking them up into a neat pile. When she was finished, she hitched up the wagon and drove to the post office. She purchased eleven stamps and carefully stuck them onto the letters. One by one, she pushed the letters through the mail slot, waiting until she heard the feathery plop as each one landed in the bin below.

Two days after Lila received the package, she went to see her doctor. He confirmed what she already knew; she was nearly three months pregnant. When Lila had begun to suspect that she was going to have a baby, she imagined how Daniel's face would look when he opened the letter announcing her pregnancy. She even let herself hope that he would send her a small gift, some little thing to let her know that he was pleased with her news. Now she wondered if she was going to have to take care of a new baby all alone, without a husband to share in the joy or the responsibility.

Every afternoon Lila walked down the long lane to the mailbox and checked to see if anyone had answered her letters. A few came back marked "addressee unknown" or "return to sender." After two months, Lila resigned herself to the idea that she was not going to receive a response to her inquiries. She waited for some official notification that Daniel was lying sick or hurt in a hospital bed somewhere or that he was dead. She needed a reason for her husband's sudden disappearance, something to contain the fear that gnawed at her, the fear that Daniel had found his old life too heavy a burden to carry and had sloughed it off for an easier life in a new place with someone else.

As Lila swelled with child, her doubts hardened into reality. Daniel was not coming home. Lila told her boys that their father was staying in the city and stopped including his name in their plans. The boys knew better than to talk about their father in front of their mother and soon he vanished from their conversations altogether. When folks in town asked about Daniel, Lila simply said that he had gone away. Hearing the tone in her voice and seeing her look of bitter disappointment, the townsfolk did not press her further about her troubles.

By the time the baby was born, Lila had relegated Daniel to the past and opened up a future that did not include him. She named the child Samuel after her father. Lila hid the abyss of her loneliness behind a wall of silence and busyness. Running a farm and caring for a newborn exhausted her to the point of numbness. When she fell into bed at night, she slept so soundly that her hidden pain could not surface in dreams.

Daniel, in his letter to Lila, had said he hoped that she would find it in her heart to forgive him, but he would understand if she could not. When he did not receive a response from her, he assumed that she found his incarceration too shameful to keep him in her life. He tried to accept the situation. Nevertheless, he found himself listening for his name to be called when the mail was delivered, wishing that Lila had had a change of heart.

Prison had a way of stripping away the dignity of a man and revealing a dark side that he didn't know was part of him. Daniel learned how to survive; he kept to himself and tried not to cause any trouble, but he sharpened his toothbrush into a knife, just in case. He developed a rigid routine to help him pass the time, dividing the long, dull days into smaller segments. To avoid thinking about the past, he developed a habit of measuring things: He counted the number of pages he read, the number of sit-ups he did, calculated how many bites he took at breakfast, added up how many steps he took around the yard. He marked the numbers on his cell wall, tallying everything up at the end of the day as a way of giving meaning to his life. Numbers replaced memories. After a time, he could no longer recall the sound of his children's voices, no longer remember what they looked like. He became hollow inside, his only goal to survive another day.

The new baby, Samuel, was content and healthy. His good-natured presence brightened the lives of Lila and her boys and gave them an excuse to exercise tenderness. As he grew older, he toddled after Tad and Simon, and they tried to make a space for him in their daily chores. Even Lila coddled the boy, allowing him to snip the blossoms off the bean plants without a reprimand.

One afternoon, when Samuel was almost three years old, he, his mother, and his two brothers attended a church supper. As they sat munching on fried chicken, Samuel looked around the table at all the mothers and fathers sitting next to each other and, in a loud voice, called out, "Where is my father?" Everyone sat in stunned silence, unable to think of what to say.

An old grandmother eased everyone's tension by looking at Samuel and saying, "Child, did I ever tell you about the time I swallowed a frog?" Samuel was so interested in her story that he forgot about his question, and everyone at the table breathed a sigh of relief.

However, Simon could not get the question out of his mind. Daniel had left when Simon was almost fifteen, a time when a young man needs the influence of his father. Lila had filled the dual roles of mother and father as best she could, but she often relied on Simon to be the "man of the house." His responsibilities had often exceeded his years; he quickly learned to make decisions and take care of himself. Daniel had always been a good and loving father, and Simon never understood his disappearance. Samuel's question caused the ache of abandonment to emerge from the recesses of Simon's heart, where he had tried to bury it. He knew he had to find out what had happened to his father.

One evening after supper, Simon asked Tad to take Samuel outside to play. When he and Lila were alone, he explained that he planned to travel into the city to see if he could find any information about his father. "I need to know why he left," Simon said. "Tad and Samuel need to know too."

Lila looked at her son's face and she could see his father's determination surface in his steadfast expression. Lila knew she could not stop him. "Go ahead," she said. "I won't stand in your way." It was as close as she could come to offering her son a blessing.

Lila went upstairs and reached into a box on her vanity where she kept a few pieces of costume jewelry to wear to church on Sunday mornings. She pulled out the earrings and necklaces, revealing a stack of old letters tied together with a ribbon at the bottom of the box. She picked one out of the pile, went back to the kitchen, and handed it to Simon. "That's the address where your father stayed in the city," she said, pointing to the corner of the envelope. Simon smiled and leaned over to kiss his mother on the cheek.

Two days later, Simon boarded a bus, checked into a hotel once he arrived in the city, and eventually came to Mrs. Johnson's boardinghouse. He introduced himself to Mrs. Johnson and asked if she remembered his father. At first, she shook her head in protest. "I meet lots of people. It's hard to remember them all," she said.

Simon continued to question her, hoping to jog her memory. "Now I remember," she exclaimed. "Yes, he seemed like a nice fellow but he got into some sort of trouble and ended up in jail. Something to do with assault, I recall." Mrs. Johnson tried but she could not summon up any more details regarding the exact nature of Daniel's difficulties.

That night, Simon lay fully dressed on his bed in the hotel, hands clasped behind his head, staring at the ceiling. He found the idea of his father sitting in a jail cell unsettling. He had always felt that his father had deserted him; now he considered the possibility that his family had forsaken his father.

Early the next day, Simon visited the courthouse and spent the entire morning hunting through the records until he found an entry for his father's case. He wrote down the name of the public defender and went to that section of the building. When he discovered that the man had joined a local law firm, he made an appointment to see him the following day.

The lawyer was very cordial but seemed surprised by Simon's investigation. "I recollect sending a package to your mother," he said. "Your father seemed like the kind of man who would have written her a letter. I'm surprised that he didn't."

"What exactly did my father do?" asked Simon.

The lawyer explained the facts of the case. "Your father didn't hurt anyone. He was just in the wrong place at the wrong time." He continued in an apologetic tone. "You see, your father was one of my first clients. I was just getting my feet wet and I didn't present his case very well. Perhaps, if I had done a better job, he wouldn't have received such a harsh sentence."

"Can I see him?" asked Simon. The lawyer helped the young man make the arrangements and wished him good luck. Simon was scheduled to visit his father the following afternoon.

Simon spent most of the night staring out his hotel window at the bright city lights, trying to sort out the confused jumble of emotions that left his stomach tied in a knot. One moment he was an angry, sorrowful teenager who desperately longed for his father's guidance. The next moment, he was a man who felt pity for his father and regretted the strange unfolding of events that had caused his family such pain. When Simon climbed into the taxi that would take him to the prison, he still had no idea what to say to his father.

When Daniel entered the visiting room, wearing his prison uniform, Simon recognized him immediately. An armed guard stood two feet away from him as he sat down at the table across from Simon. Daniel looked at him. "Simon?" he whispered after a moment.

"Yes, Dad, it's me," replied his son. "How are you?"

"I'm okay," answered Daniel.

The words were hollow containers, unable to convey all the feelings that roiled around inside father and son. Silence offered safety and neither man spoke again for a few moments.

Daniel stared at his hands, then lifted his head and croaked, "How's your mother?" Simon opened his mouth and four years of history and emotion started to pour out. Daniel leaned forward, trying to navigate the stream of information, interrupting with a question now and again so that he could get his bearings. When Simon mentioned his baby brother, Daniel begged him for all the details, asking, "I have another son? What's his name? What does he look like?"

Finally, the question that Simon had carried around with him since his father's departure erupted. "Why didn't you let us know what had happened?"

Daniel was stunned. He leaned back in his chair as if a wave had knocked him over. He recalled the hours it had taken him to write that letter, how he had struggled to find the right words, words that let Lila know how sorry he was, how much he was going to miss her and the boys. "I wrote a letter to your mother. I gave it to the lawyer to put in the box with my other things," he said.

It was Simon's turn to be taken aback. "She got the box but there was no letter in it. Mom wrote letters to the boardinghouse and the other addresses in your pockets. No one ever answered them. We never knew what happened." The full weight of this revelation was too much to take in all at once. Daniel and Simon were unable to speak.

"You've got two minutes," the guard informed them.

Neither father nor son wanted to say good-bye; the connection between them seemed too fragile to bear another separation. They stood up and shook hands. "I'll be back," promised Simon. He watched Daniel leave and remained standing, staring at the door, long after his father had gone away.

Simon took the first bus back home. He needed to spill out this perplexing news, needed someone to help him make sense of it all. He arrived late at night and walked up the lane in the dark, causing the dogs to bark and waking his mother out of a sound sleep. When Lila ran downstairs and saw her son, she braced herself for the worst. "What's the matter, Simon?" she asked.

"Let's sit down and have a cup of coffee," suggested Simon. "I've got a lot to tell you." They sat together at the kitchen table until the early hours of the morning, sipping coffee out of thick white mugs, while Simon relayed the whole story to his mother. As Lila listened to each new clue, the hidden dread that had held her bound for so many years slowly loosened its hold.

When Simon finished the last detail, Lila stared at her son in disbelief. "After all these years," she said, her voice trailing off. One by one, tears began to dribble down her face as she repeatedly whispered, "He didn't leave me, he didn't leave me."

Daniel sat in his cell that night puzzling over the strangeness of things. A few years back, such a turn of events would have angered him and galvanized him into action. Time and circumstance had tempered his sense of autonomy; he recognized his inability to regulate fortune's path. Now it was enough that his family had not forgotten him. He allowed gratefulness to wash over him and restore feeling to his numbed heart.

The next Thursday, Lila, Simon, Tad, and Samuel came to visit Daniel. Lila reached out and touched her husband for the first time in four years. Tenderly, she picked up his hand and kissed his fingertips one by one. Daniel kissed her forehead, the familiar scent of her presence bringing tears to his eyes. He welcomed Tad and Simon, shaking their hands and clapping them on the shoulders. Lila introduced Samuel to his father, placing the child on Daniel's lap. Tad and Simon watched as their father repeated a game from their childhood, his old trick of wiggling his ears while keeping his face perfectly still. They all smiled as Samuel laughed and said, "Do it again!"

Daniel had three months left in prison. He stopped counting pages and sit-ups, replacing those figures with the days and hours remaining until he was reunited with his family. Every night he drew a cross over another day until the black slashes eclipsed the numerals and one number stood alone.

On the morning of his release, the last thing Daniel did was draw a line through that number, validating his emancipation. Simon met his father at the prison gate with a bus ticket in his hand. They sat together in the back seat of the bus, Daniel staring out the window the entire time, watching the landscape pass by, trying to convince himself that his confinement had finally ended.

When the bus driver dropped them off at the end of their lane, Daniel looked around, took a deep breath, and inhaled the scent of freshly cut hay. "I'm home, Simon," he said. "I'm home at last!"

Lila, Tad, and Samuel were waiting for them on the front porch. When Daniel saw his wife, he ran to her, wrapped his arms around her, and kissed her deeply. Arm in arm, they walked into the kitchen, and the entire family settled themselves around the table to enjoy Daniel's favorite meal, a chicken dinner with all the trimmings. They passed bowls and platters, heaping their plates with mashed potatoes, stuffing, carrots, and green beans. They started to eat and Daniel bent his head, shoveling the food into his mouth. After a few bites, he realized that his time was not rationed, and he leaned back in his chair, savoring each delicious mouthful. When they went to bed, Daniel and Lila talked and touched and held one another tightly all through the night, each afraid that if they let go the other would disappear.

It took time for Daniel to slip free of his prison habits. Working side by side with Tad and Simon helped, the routine daily chores easing him back into the rhythm of life on the farm. In Daniel's absence, Tad and Simon had assumed much of the responsibility for running the farm and there was less for Daniel to do. He spent the time getting to know Samuel, his youngest child. The two of them fished in the pond, fed the chickens, and tended Lila's enormous garden, pulling weeds and picking vegetables. Daniel listened with delight to Samuel's unceasing chatter as he marveled at everything he saw, the child's presence restoring his confidence in the goodness of this world. Day by day, joy crept back into that household.

One evening, as they sat around the table, Daniel reached into his pocket and pulled out his gold watch. Looking at his oldest son, he held out the watch, saying, "Simon, I want you to have this. My father gave it to me on my twenty-first birthday. I feel you deserve it. You came and found me. You brought me back to life. If it wasn't for you, I might not be here today."

Simon took the watch, cradled it in his palm, and rubbed its shiny surface. "Thank you," he said, and then he looked over at his father. "If it is all the same to you, I'm going to hold onto it for Samuel until he is ready. I think he should have it. You see, Samuel broke the silence. He asked where you were and made me remember. He kept you from being forgotten." Everyone at the table smiled because they all knew that it was true.

Our family stories help us discover who we are; they place us in a system of relationships that connect us to the past and situate us in the present. As we sit around the dinner table or in our grandmother's parlor and share our experiences, we compose, along with our listeners, a personal narrative that helps us make sense of our lives. Shaping family history is a continuous process. As we weave

new pieces of information into the story and retell it, we gradually reshape the context of our lives, and our identity becomes richer and more complex.

Drastic life changes, such as divorce, death, imprisonment, moving, or job loss, alter the structure of the family, making us feel as if the underpinnings of our world have come loose. As we try to fit into new roles and adapt to different situations, we often reconsider our family history. We seek new information, unlock secrets, and probe deeper into existing stories as we search for clues to help us understand our changed responsibilities. Sometimes, the old stories are no longer sufficient; they do not explain what has happened. We explore alternative ways of looking at things; we ask questions, emphasize different parts of the story, and arrive at other conclusions. Our personal narrative shifts as we layer new meaning onto old happenings. As we tell this version of the story, we learn to live our lives in a new way. We are no longer trapped by past assumptions if we remember to ask the simple questions that reveal the great truths of love, family, and spirit.

14

The Junkyard Refuge

A Kazakh Folktale Retold

Will recognized danger as soon as he heard the rumble of heavy feet on the iron grating of the bridge overhead. Grabbing the knapsack containing all his earthly possessions, he rushed out of the ramshackle camp just as the sentry banged two tin pots together and sounded the alarm, "Run! Run, it's the governor's men!" Will scuttled over the embankment toward the road that ran beneath the rusty bridge. Out of concern, he hesitated for a moment and turned to see the police, their nightsticks raised, charge into the pitiful cluster of shacks tucked next to the buttress of the bridge. He watched the people scatter to avoid being rousted and dragged away. He could do nothing to help.

Since taking up residence in the city's most elegant mansion two years ago, the governor had started a rigorous program of renewal, razing the poorer neighborhoods and constructing stylish new buildings for tenants who were more prosperous. Their homes destroyed, the poor were forced to become squatters, living in the streets or in abandoned buildings. The presence of the destitute offended the wealthy, and they complained to the governor, who, in an effort to appease them, periodically sent out his troops to force the impoverished out of the streets and out of sight.

When the governor had started his renovation project, Will's best friend, Everton, had warned him, "There's going to be trouble. I'm going to get out of here while the getting is good. Why don't you come with me?"

Will dismissed his misgivings with a laugh. "You're nothing but an old worrywart, Everton," he had said.

Everton had packed his bags and moved outside the city limits. A month later, Will received a letter from his friend, saying that he had found a safe place to live and extending an invitation to Will. "The door's open ... come whenever you can!" Below the invitation, he had painstakingly drawn a map to show Will the way.

As Will crouched with his back against the wall of a crumbling building, he reached into the inside pocket of his jacket, pulled out the letter, and read it for the hundredth time. He had been living hand to mouth for well over a year, scavenging for food, shifting in and out of vagrant settlements, and trying to salvage some hope that things would get better. He studied the map carefully. It would take him the better part of three days to walk to Everton's place, and he would have to make it through some seamy and desolate areas. He looked around at the vacant warehouses and empty lots littered with broken bottles. The dismal landscape offered no sign of encouragement. Will put the map back in his pocket, hitched his knapsack more tightly on his shoulder, and started off through the deserted streets.

Hours later he arrived at the riverfront and stopped to rest, sitting on the sun-warmed cement of the bulwark and dangling his legs over the edge. As he looked at the water gently lapping against the cement, a mellow voice inquired, "Mind if I join you?" Will looked up quickly; he did not like to be caught off guard by strangers. A slightly built, white-haired woman stood looking down at him. She wore a jacket, overalls, and scuffed work boots, but carried no purse or other belongings.

"Go ahead," said Will warily. He was surprised at how nimbly the woman moved, plopping herself down with ease and sitting cross-legged.

The old woman reached into her oversized pocket, pulled out an apple, and burnished it against the sleeve of her jacket until its red skin glistened in the sun. Will stared. He hadn't eaten fresh fruit since his eviction. "Where'd you get that?" he blurted out.

"I have my ways," she smiled, her eyes twinkling in the sunlight. She pulled out a small pearl-handled penknife, cut the apple in two, and offered half to Will. "Go ahead," she said. "You look hungry."

Will grabbed the apple and began to chomp noisily. Only after he had taken several bites did the memory of etiquette surface and, with his mouth full, he stammered out a watery thank-you.

"Not a problem," she replied. The old woman placed her piece of apple on the cement, reached into her other pocket, pulled out a bag of bread, and began to toss morsels into the river. Soon gulls circled above the water and dove down to grab the bread. She picked up her apple and began to nibble. "It's nice to have company when you eat," she said, tossing more bread upon the water. She turned to Will and held out the bag, saying, "Would you like to feed them?"

Tentatively, he took the bag and tossed out a bit of bread. Will had endured the harshness of life on the streets by numbing his sympathy toward others; it was as if his heart had fallen asleep. Now this every-day expression of generosity created a tingling awareness of the price he had paid for survival. Slowly, he continued to fling scraps to the birds, watching the delicate arc of the bread.

"What brings you to these parts?" asked the woman.

"I'm heading north." Will described his trek based on Everton's map.

"Rubbish Hills," she said in surprise. "Not too many people travel there."

"Why do you call it Rubbish Hills?"

"When they tore down the old neighborhoods, the governor's crew hauled the wreckage away to various places—I guess he didn't want the leftovers of the unfortunate to clutter up the domain of the rich. Some of the rubble was taken up north to an empty field nick-named Rubbish Hills. I didn't know anybody lived up there."

Will briefly explained Everton's letter. "I'm glad you have a friend," said the woman in a tender voice. "Everyone needs someone to belong to, someplace where they feel safe. People have trouble finding their souls in loneliness and struggle. The best part of them gets covered up in fear and contempt." She reached back into her pocket, brought out the pearl penknife and handed it to Will. "Here. Take this. It will help you along the way!"

In Will's world, exchanges of this magnitude did not take place without haggling or the demand of reciprocity. "Are you sure?" he said.

The old woman simply nodded her head and placed the knife in Will's outstretched hand. Will cradled the knife in his palm, feeling its silky smoothness and watching the pearl handle as it gleamed in the sunlight. When he lifted his head to extend his heartfelt thanks to the silver-haired woman, she had disappeared. However, resting on the cement where she sat was another ruby-red apple.

Will's journey took less time than he had thought and was graced with an unaccustomed ease. He came upon a family of squatters who willingly traded a cup of thin soup for slices of fresh apple. As he cut the apple into sections with his knife, he readily shared in the family's conversation and listened to their stories. Farther along, he found a deserted lean-to that kept a chill night wind at bay. His encounter with the old woman lingered in his mind and brightened his thoughts of the future. The pearl-handled knife, nestled in the bottom of his pocket, was a concrete reminder of her presence and his talisman of hope.

Will had no difficulty recognizing his destination. Rubbish Hills consisted of several huge piles of debris dumped in a circle in the middle of a grassy field. He walked around the towering mounds of wreckage. Doorframes, wooden beams, bricks, twisted window sashes, old tires, and iron fencing were all massed together, discarded fragments of a hundred individual households muddled together in a crumpled heap. He stepped between two piles and walked toward the large open center of the dump, looking for signs of Everton. In front of a scrap heap, he saw a tiny, hodgepodge house. Two mismatched windows and a thick wooden door peeked out of a patchwork-brick and cement-block façade, topped by a pointed metal roof with a stovepipe chimney. Will gave a wry smile when he noticed that Everton had put the house number 1163 on his front door and placed an old mailbox to the left of the front step. Apparently, he still had a sense of humor. Will knocked, and in a few moments, Everton opened the door. His eyes widened when he saw his old friend and he bellowed with great joy, "Well, will you look at what the cat dragged in!" Then he reached out and embraced Will. "Come on in," he said. "You're just in time for lunch."

The heady aroma of fried fish and onions filled the open space that served as kitchen, dining, and living rooms. The long-forgotten trappings of domesticity—silverware, a table with chairs, and a plant in an old tin can resting on the windowsill—welcomed Will and he exclaimed in delight, "This is wonderful!"

"I'd try a couple of bites before I offered that opinion," said Everton, placing a plate of fish, potatoes, and onions in front of Will.

Will shoveled the food into his mouth, and closed his eyes as he savored the taste. He tried to balance his hunger against his curiosity. As they ate, he realized that Everton was as eager for conversation as he was for food; he listened as Everton described his life in the junkyard.

"When I left my home in the neighborhood, I knew I wasn't coming back. I packed up everything I thought I would need to start a new life. I took all my tools, plants, even the seeds and seedlings for my plot in the community garden, and stuffed them into the car and drove away," explained Everton.

"How did you find this place?"

"It was by accident, really. When I left, I didn't have a specific destination in mind. I knew I had to leave the city and I thought I might find a place in the country. I stopped at a gas station to ask directions. This strange old man with wild silver hair appeared out of nowhere and said he knew of a place called Rubbish Hills that might have what I was looking for. He gave me the route and I ended up here!

"I saw these huge piles and they seemed pretty interesting, so I parked the car and started snooping around. I made my way into the center and just stood there. There was this big open space surrounded by these mountains of junk and I got this strange feeling that I was protected somehow. That all this stuff that had been ripped out of people's lives wasn't just garbage ... that there was still some spirit from the old neighborhoods present and I wasn't alone. I drove the car in and set up housekeeping."

"What you've built is pretty amazing. It must have been a lot of hard work," said Will.

"Yeah, it has been a lot of work. But there is a kind of magic in this place. Any time I need something, I just start digging in these piles and it surfaces. I've come across lots of things. Olive oil, for instance. I found an entire case of those big rectangular cans. I have enough olive oil to last me a lifetime! I've found candles, blankets, tools. Whenever I need something, I just start digging and, sooner or later, I find it. Sometimes, I even find things I don't know I need. One time, I was feeling pretty lonely, being here all by myself. Two days later, I found a box of books. I spent my nights reading and I didn't feel so alone anymore.

"What about you, Will? I've gone on long enough. Tell me about yourself."

"I'm not sure there is much to tell," Will said as he leaned back in his chair. "I stayed in the old neighborhood until they evicted me. I never thought such a thing could happen. I wasn't the only one; there were lots of us. We kept hoping things would get better but they never did. Once the neighborhood was gone, it was as if goodwill and kindness vanished as well. It isn't easy to survive on the streets. I did things I never thought I could do. I begged, fought, stole. A little bit of me disappeared every day until I wasn't sure I recognized myself anymore. There was no place where I felt safe. There was no one to remind me of who I was ... except you, Everton. Without your letter, I don't know what would have happened to me."

"I worried about you after I left. The idea of the letter came to me in a dream. I couldn't ignore it. I woke up early in the morning, sat down, and wrote out a map. There was still gas left in the car then, so I drove to a post office I remembered seeing and mailed you the letter. I always hoped you would show up."

The two friends sat in silence, pondering the incredible way their lives intertwined. Finally, Everton stood up and said, "Come on, let me show you around. What you see in here is what there is," he said, waving his hand around the room. Outside, he pointed out the terrace he had made from old floorboards and iron railings. Will looked at the makeshift chairs and table and out over the railing to a patch of cultivated ground. "I see you're able to grow a garden," he said.

"Sure am," replied Everton. "This was an empty meadow before they filled it with rubbish. Lucky for me, the soil is good and things seem to grow well. It keeps me well fed all year round. I have plenty of food during the summer—tomatoes, squash, beans, peas—and I'm also able to store cabbages, turnips, potatoes, and onions for the winter. And, of course, I have my herbs and flowers. I love this garden; it helps me feel as if I'm connected to something larger than myself." Everton led Will out of the junkyard, through a grassy field edged with berry bushes toward a little lake—"Spring-fed, it never goes dry," he explained. "I'm able to draw water from here all year round. It's also my fish market. I caught our lunch here!"

After a few days, Everton and Will developed an equitable division of labor, each choosing chores suited to his own personality and individual abilities. Will relaxed into the comfort of domestic routine. The predictable rhythm of his days was a welcome contrast to the chaotic frenzy of his life in the streets and eased his ragged spirit. He no longer spent his nights sleeping with one eye open to avoid danger. Instead, he slumbered so deeply that his dreams returned.

One day, as Will sorted through one of the trash heaps in search of firewood, he spotted something bright and shiny poking out of the debris. He pushed away the litter and pulled out a small tin box, ornately painted gold and red, with a tiny lock in the front. Will fiddled with the lock, but had no success in opening the box. That evening, he showed it to Everton. "Let me get a screwdriver," said Everton. "I'll have it open in a jiffy."

"Wait," said Will. "It's such a pretty box. I would hate to bend it by prying it open. Maybe I can pick the lock with my penknife." He pulled the knife out of his pocket and inserted the blade into the lock. After a few seconds of tinkering, the lid sprang wide open, revealing several large stacks of $10 and $20 bills. Will gave out a low whistle and Everton a loud shout when they saw the contents of the box.

"There's got to be a fortune in there," said Everton.

The two men counted the money—twice, just to make sure they had counted right. They were flabbergasted by how much money had been tucked into that little box—over $2,000. "That's a lot of money. What are we going to do with it all?" asked Will.

"It's a lot of responsibility, Will. Don't get me wrong, I'm willing to spend it. There is part of me that wants to have one heck of a party. But, as I've said before, those heaps out there have a certain kind of magic. I can't help feeling that this money has been given to us so that we can do something special with it."

"But what?"

"I don't know," said Everton. "We'll just have to think about it and trust that the answer will come to one of us."

The next three days were quiet ones for Will and Everton. They worked silently, poring over the possibilities the money offered them. As they ate their supper, they tossed ideas back and forth, but nothing seemed quite satisfactory. On the third night, Will looked at his old friend and said, "Everton, I have given a lot of thought to this whole thing. Today as I was working, the sun was beating down on my back. I was hot and the sweat poured down my face and neck. I said to myself, 'What I wouldn't give for a little shade right now.' And it hit me, Everton, we don't have any trees here. Back in the old neighborhood, I used to love to go to the park, sit on a bench underneath a tree and watch the people go by. It was so restful to the spirit. Everton, we need to plant trees."

Everton jumped up and slapped his hand on the tabletop. "That's perfect! We can plant a park, a haven of green right in the middle of a junkyard."

"And wouldn't it be great if some of the street people came to the park? Just for a little while, just long enough to remember who they really are!"

The two men sat up late, talking and making plans. They pushed aside the furniture and Everton took a piece of charred wood from the stove. Using a combination of his and Will's ideas, he drew a plan on the floor so they both could see what the park would look like. Each man recalled his favorite trees from the park and together they determined what trees they should buy. They decided that Will would take the money to the flower market at the edge of the city, where he would purchase as many saplings as they could afford and he could carry.

The next morning, Will and Everton walked around the open space in the center of the junkyard and marked all the places where they would need to dig holes for the trees. They developed a pattern of several small groves separated by pathways that converged near the garden. During the next two weeks, they worked from early in the morning until dusk, turning over the soil, hauling away rocks and digging holes. When the soil was prepared and all the holes dug, Will spent some time getting ready for his journey to the city. He memorized the route that he would take and sewed special pockets on the inside of his shirt to keep the money safe from thieves and pickpockets. As he carefully stitched the pockets in place, he relived the misery of his days on the street, trying to brace himself for what might happen when he returned.

Unable to sleep, Will got up before dawn on the day he was to leave. He took his knapsack and packed food, a blanket, some string, and several pieces of cloth to soak in water to keep the roots of the trees moist on the return trip. He put the money inside his shirt and made sure that his lucky penknife was in his trousers pocket. While Will packed, Everton fried up some potatoes and onions for breakfast. Neither man spoke as they slowly chewed their food, each afraid to shatter the safety of silence by voicing the shape and form of their worries. When they finished eating, Will donned his backpack and made his way to the front door. Everton followed him. "Good luck, my friend," he said. "I'll see you in a few days." Will put out his hand. Everton grabbed it with both of his hands and once more offered his blessing, "Good luck!" Will walked across the freshly turned earth and disappeared from sight around the edge of a pile of trash.

From his days on the street, Will remembered several good hiding places where he could sleep at night and stay out of harm's way. He no longer had to beg for food. He started his travels each morning just as the first light brightened the sky.

On the morning of the third day, Will passed through a district of one-story warehouses and arrived at the flower market, a vast lot lined with row upon row of unusual cut flowers and exotic potted plants. As he looked for the area reserved for trees, he saw well-dressed designers sashaying through the aisles, telling clerks which plants to load into trucks for their wealthy clients. When he found the section with trees rooted in black plastic pots, he searched for saplings and examined the tags in an effort to find the trees he and Everton had chosen.

A proprietor dressed in a fashionable ensemble approached Will. She raised her eyebrows at his dirty fingernails and worn clothes, and inquired in a clipped tone, "May I help you?" Will was about to risk explaining his mission when an earsplitting shriek pierced the dull prattle of the marketplace.

Will turned toward the sound and saw a truck with horizontal wooden slats parked by the curb. A mournful screech followed a pitiful trill, one after the other, until an entire chorus of lamentation emanated from the truck. The sound touched a nerve inside Will and he ran toward the vehicle. Peering into the back, Will saw dozens of wire cages filled with birds, each one containing a prime specimen. There was a slender, elegant bird with a white crest, copper plumage, and long tail feathers of emerald and burgundy. A swan the color of black velvet looped his graceful neck around and tucked his head under a wing edged in crimson. There was a goose with dusky blue feathers sporting a knobbed, pumpkin-colored beak, exotic ducks of all kinds, and a pair of rose-colored pigeons nestled next to each other. They were the most beautiful birds Will had ever seen.

The driver of the truck had stopped to purchase breakfast from a pushcart vendor on the corner. He threw the crumpled paper wrapping from his food onto the sidewalk, opened the door of his truck, and stepped up into the cab.

"Where are you taking those birds?" demanded Will.

Through his open window, the driver looked down at Will. "Not that it's any of your business, guttersnipe, but these birds are destined for the governor's dinner table. It seems he's developed a taste for rare fowl."

"No," cried Will. "You can't ..." His voice trailed off.

"Can and will. The governor pays a pretty penny for these birds."

"I can pay," Will said. "I've got money." He reached under his shirt, pulled forth a stack of bills, and waved them in front of the truck driver.

The man laughed. "That's hardly enough!"

"There's plenty more where that came from."

The man cocked his head to one side as he judged Will's sincerity. "All right, meet me over there. We'll see what we can do," he said, pointing his finger to an alleyway across the street. He maneuvered the truck across the street and backed it into the alleyway.

Will and the driver negotiated for some time. The governor had deep pockets and it took all the money Will had to ransom the captive birds. When Will and the driver finished unloading the cages onto the ground, the driver turned to Will and said, "So, what are you going to do with these birds?"

"Set them free," Will replied.

"What!" exclaimed the driver. "You mean to tell me that you just paid all that money so that you can set them free? Why would you do such a thing?"

Will wasn't sure that he understood it himself. He stammered a reply. "They're beautiful. Too beautiful to be used up and thrown away. They should be appreciated for what they are, allowed to become what they were meant to be."

The driver shook his head in disbelief. "Well, it's your money. You can spend it any way you want. But, by the looks of you, you've got better ways to spend it," and he started to get into his truck. He hesitated for a moment, then turned around, looked Will right in the eye, and said, "Good luck."

Will rushed from cage to cage, undoing latches and opening the doors to freedom. Released from their confinement, the creatures cautiously stepped into the alley and stretched their cramped wings to their fullest span, adjusting to the unfamiliar breadth of space. Slowly, they began to beat their wings, feeling the old rhythm return. With a joyous whir, the birds rose into the air and flew away, a vibrant feathery blanket fluttering through the sky.

Will ran through the streets, face upturned, following the flight of the birds until they were nothing but a distant speck in the sky. Then he started the journey back to the junkyard. At first, Will felt elated and skipped along, reliving the moment of triumph when he had set the birds free. However, as the days wore on, his exhilaration ebbed and he regretted his impulsiveness. Everton had trusted him with their money and their dream. "How am I going to face Everton?" he thought to himself. "How can I return empty-handed?"

Will stumbled into the junkyard as the evening sun enveloped the dump in a warm, coppery glow. The empty holes lay before him, a silent reprimand for his impetuous action. Everton stood in the center of the yard, his back to Will, lost in thought. Will's heart sank when he realized that Everton was envisioning how the place would look when the trees were grown.

In a trembling voice, he called out, "I'm home, Everton."

Everton immediately swung around, a smile of relief crossing his face. "Will, thank heaven, you're safe. Did you get the trees?"

"No, I didn't," mumbled Will.

Everton examined his friend's regretful face and said, "You look tired. Come inside. I'll fix you something to eat and you can tell me all about it."

Will washed up and changed his clothes while Everton fixed supper. As they ate, Will tried to put into words his reaction to the trapped birds and explain why he had bought their freedom. "I'm sorry, Everton," he apologized. "I didn't mean to let you down."

"It's okay. I understand," said Everton with sympathy. "I would have done the same thing."

Exhausted from his trek, Will went to bed immediately after he finished eating his meal. Everton stayed up. He tidied up the kitchen, made himself a cup of herb tea, then sat down at the table and tried to sort through his jumbled feelings. He was about to go to bed when he heard a strange rustling sound that grew louder and louder until it sounded like a great wind blowing through the junkyard.

Everton looked out the window and when he saw what was making the noise, he ran to get Will. "Wake up!" he shouted, shaking his slumbering friend. "Come on. You've got to see what's happening."

Everton raced to the terrace as Will sluggishly followed behind. The two men stared at the area that had been prepared for the trees; it was filled with birds. Some of the birds Will recognized as those he had set free and he pointed them out to Everton. However, he could not identify many others. In the pale moonlight, the mass of fluttering birds resembled a shimmering, quivering cloud. Each bird carried a sprig of green in its beak. One by one, the birds placed their tiny shoots into the holes, and the twigs took root. Slender saplings emerged, growing taller and thicker, stretching out branches that sprouted delicate yellow-green buds. The buds quickly blossomed into clusters of pearl-colored flowers edged with shiny little leaves. The foliage coarsened on each tree, the petals shivered to the ground, and the branches bore apples and pears of every variety. As the early-morning sky brightened, the birds flew into the trees and began to warble a joyous symphony while a fountain bubbled up in the center of the orchard. Will and Everton stepped off the terrace and into the grove. They ran their hands over the tree trunks, feeling the roughness of the bark, and they reached up to pluck apples and pears from the overhanging branches.

"Have you ever tasted anything so good?" said Will to Everton.

"No, I never have," he replied. "I told you this place has a special kind of magic." All morning long, they strolled along the pathways between the trees, marveling at the wondrous event that had taken place right under their noses.

The next day, a ragged husband and wife wandered into the junk-yard with their baby girl. Will saw them standing amid the trees and as he approached them, he overheard their astounded murmurs. "It's true, it's really, really true!"

"What do you mean?" he asked.

"My wife had a dream about a garden of peace where we could be safe for a while," replied the man.

Seeing their gaunt, worn-out features, Will offered them the hospitality of the orchard. "Welcome," he said. "Rest yourselves and eat all you want. There is plenty." The couple picked a few apples and some pears. They sat in the shade of one of the trees and nibbled the fruit, allowing the tension in their weary bodies to trickle out with every bite. The woman cradled her baby in her arms and fell asleep while nursing the child, her head nestled in the crook of her husband's arm. Will observed them from a distance, knowing that his presence would disrupt their retreat. Later, when he stopped back to check on the family, they were gone.

Whispers carried word of the junkyard orchard softly through the settlement camps, holding out a promise of renewal to the destitute. Only those with tender hearts and good intentions bothered to make the difficult journey. One by one, they straggled into the grove, some staying for a few days, others for a week or two. They remained long enough to allow goodness and generosity to soothe their frayed spirits, then they returned to the streets with that memory alive in their hearts.

Rumors of this strange and wondrous garden reached the governor's mansion and he sent out his mounted police to investigate. The patrol traveled northward, the horses' hooves pounding the earth and causing it to tremble from the force. As the unit rode through fields of grass toward the junkyard, the magical heaps shuddered and loosened the barbed wire and iron fences hidden within them. The wire tumbled in steep coils between the piles and the fences closed in the gaps, erecting an impenetrable barricade. The company galloped round and round the mountains of garbage, but never found an entryway. "Nothing but a wild goose chase!" declared the captain.

"It's ridiculous to think that anything worthwhile could be found in this pile of rubble." The troops returned to the governor and reported that no such place existed; the garden was nothing but lies and nonsense. The barrier of fence and wire dissolved when the police departed, but the orchard remained. Concealed within the mountains of rubbish, here was a place where the poor and neglected could seek refuge, reclaim their identity, and realize the integrity of their true nature.

The word paradise *comes from the Persian word* pairi-daeza, *meaning "enclosed space." In ancient times, skilled Persian architects designed elegant gardens to provide shelter from the windswept desert and the scorching sun. Protected from a harsh climate behind walls or rows of trees, the delicate combination of colorful plantings and tranquil pools offered people emotional sanctuary and an opportunity for leisurely relaxation. The peace and harmony of these "earthly paradises" allowed for contemplation and became a window to the inner life, reminding people that God is the source of all beauty.*

The practice of tending a garden connects us to the eternal rhythms of life. By nurturing plants through the seasonal cycles of growth and decay, we touch upon the mysteries of death and rebirth. We sense the fragility of our own lives as well as the transcendence of things. This intimacy with creative energy expands our awareness and we pause for a moment in wonder as we experience the vastness and beauty of this marvelous universe.

15

The Gift

A Tale from the Beta Israel Jews
of Ethiopia Retold

*L*ong ago, there lived a poor, hardworking farmer who believed each day was a gift from God. He followed the rhythm of the land, sowing and harvesting, according to the seasons. He had experienced both abundance and drought, but did not let difficult times blind him to the beauty of the world. He delighted in the busy hum of the bees, enjoyed a cool breeze at the end of a hot day, and marveled at the resilience of the fragile butterflies that skittered across his field.

Early one morning, the farmer walked to his field and began to cut grain. He labored until the intense heat of the noonday sun required him to seek the shelter of a nearby apple tree. As he reclined in the dappled shade, he glanced up and saw the most incredible apple dangling from the branch of the tree. It was larger than all the other apples and its unblemished ruby skin gleamed in the sunlight. His first thought was to share its beauty with his wife and daughter. He reached up and gently twisted the stem, and the apple fell right into his hand.

He raced home, rushed into the kitchen, and carefully placed the apple in the center of the table. Inviting his wife and daughter to view his treasure, he said, "Look at this. Isn't this the most splendid apple you have ever seen?"

His wife bent her head to inspect the fruit. "Indeed, it is impressive," she agreed.

The farmer's daughter tenderly picked up the apple and held it toward the light, turning it from one side to the other as she studied its perfect form and glistening skin. "It is a blessing from God," she finally declared.

The farmer looked at the lovely young woman who had brightened his life in so many ways. "Take it," he said. "It is yours."

"Oh, no," said his daughter without pause. "I can't. It is fit for a king." And she handed the apple to her father.

"That's it, my child. You are absolutely right. It is fit for a king. Tomorrow I will bring this to the palace and offer it to the king."

The next morning, the farmer bid his wife and daughter farewell, and began his journey to the royal city. He carried with him some food, water, and the apple, wrapped up in a clean, soft cloth. As he walked along the hot, dusty road, the flies buzzed around his head, but they did not bother him. His heart danced for joy because he was able to offer the king a worthy gift.

After two days, the farmer arrived at the edge of the city and made his way through the crowded streets until he came to the palace gates. Two uniformed soldiers stood on either side of the gate, guarding the entrance. "Excuse me," said the farmer. "I have a gift for the king."

The guards stared at the humble farmer, his plain clothes and sandaled feet covered with dust from his travels. "What could you possibly have that the king would want?" said one.

The farmer reached into his pack, pulled out the apple, unwrapping it to show the soldier. It was still as fresh and beautiful as the day it was picked. The other sentry shook his head and laughed. "The king has an orchard of his own with hundreds of apples."

"He doesn't have an apple like this one," said the farmer. "Please, let me in. I must give him this apple." The farmer pleaded with the guards until they summoned their commander. He examined the apple and observed that it was a perfect specimen. He listened to the farmer's explanation and was touched by the sincerity of his offering. "It is a fitting tribute to our majesty," he declared and escorted the farmer to the king's chambers.

As the farmer made his way through the hallways of the palace, a tingle of anticipation wriggled inside as he thought to himself, "I do hope the king likes the gift." The commander of the guards introduced the farmer to the king. The farmer bowed low and then, unable to stem the rush of his words, blurted out, "I found this apple in a tree on my farm. It is the most beautiful apple I have ever seen. You have been such a good king and I wanted to give you a gift worthy of your kindness." The farmer straightened up and stretched out his hands. "I hope you like it."

The king was accustomed to the ceremonial formality that accompanied the required gifts from visiting dignitaries. The farmer's straightforward gesture of devotion moved him greatly. He took the apple from the farmer's hands and stared in wonder at its simple perfection. "It's beautiful," he said and motioned for the queen to look at it. Moved by her husband's enthusiasm, she nodded and said, "It is extraordinary!"

The farmer smiled with deep pleasure and satisfaction.

"My good man," said the king, "a gift as wonderful and rare as this deserves a gift in return."

"Oh no, Your Majesty," replied the farmer. "That is not why I came."

"I realize that," said the king. "I seldom receive gifts without strings attached. Please allow me to show my gratitude. Did you walk here from your farm in the country?"

"Yes, Your Majesty," answered the farmer.

"Then you shall ride home!" He turned to one of his servants. "Have the stable master saddle up one of my finest stallions and bring it into the courtyard."

Overjoyed by his good fortune, the farmer repeatedly thanked everyone he saw. All the way home, as he trotted along, he sang the praises of the king and God above.

Like feathers in the wind, word spread throughout the city until everyone knew that the king had given one of his finest horses to a simple farmer in return for an apple. A greedy merchant heard the news and began to scheme. "If the king gave the farmer a horse for an apple, I wonder what he would give me?" He paced back and forth, muttering to himself, "Suppose I gave the king a horse, maybe he would give me jewels or silver or gold."

The merchant saddled the finest horse in his stable and rode it to the palace. He explained to the guards that he had brought the king a gift. Taking note of his fine clothes and stately bearing, the sentries quickly ushered him into the king's chambers. When the merchant saw the king on his throne, he bowed low, then hastily stood up and announced his gift. "Your Majesty, when I heard of the farmer's simple gift, I was inspired. I decided to bring you a gift as well. I have brought you the best stallion in my stable."

"Thank you, your gift is much appreciated," said the king, nodding his head and returning to his deliberations. The merchant shuffled his feet, but made no move to leave the room. The king looked up. "Is there something else?" he asked. The merchant coughed politely and began to stammer.

"I see," said the king. "You are waiting for a gift in return." The king thought for a moment. "Very well, a gift in return it shall be. I will give you something precious and valuable, something to match the pedigree of your stallion." The king leaned over and whispered instructions to one of his servants.

As the merchant waited, he grew more and more excited, thinking of the possible gifts the king might bestow upon him. When the servant returned, he carried a silver tray in his hands. Sitting on the tray was a perfectly formed, shiny red apple. The servant extended the tray toward the merchant.

"This is all I get for my troubles?" shrieked the merchant. "A plain, ordinary apple!"

The king responded. "It is no ordinary apple. It is very special, for a man who expected nothing in return gave it to me. It was a gift from the heart. There is no better gift in all the world."

We give gifts for many reasons: social obligation, charitable donations, as part of holiday celebrations, to honor someone special. At times, this practice of giving carries with it a sense of reciprocity—we give in direct measure to what we have received or in accordance with our ability. There are also times when we give a gift simply to make another person happy.

Gratitude for the blessings we have in our lives can prompt us to share with others. We realize that our good fortune is not attributable to anything we have done or deserve—it is a gift from the Divine and meant to be shared. We acknowledge the earth's bounty and the gifts we have received by giving back some of what we have to the world around us. We share our talents, give of our time, and contribute our material wealth to those in need. These gifts are offerings from the heart, sincere messages to those we care about, indicating who we think they are and recognizing their special presence in our lives. There are times, though, when the needs of a particular group of people are so great that an individual cannot alleviate their difficulties. Often, in such times, another group collectively reaches out to offer assistance. Such was the case of the Jews in Ethiopia in the 1980s.

The Jews of Ethiopia, considered by some to be one of the "lost tribes" of Israel, have a long, complex history and are commonly referred to as the Falasha, although Beta Israel is their proper appellation. The civil war and famine of the 1980s prompted the evacuation of Ethiopian Jews to Israel, organized and funded by the generosity of Jews already in Israel and around the world. From September 1984 to March 1985, Operation Moses airlifted to Israel fifteen thousand Jews from Sudanese refugee camps where they had fled to escape starvation. In 1991, Operation Solomon flew twenty thousand more directly from Ethiopia to Israel. Israel believed they had rescued all Ethiopian Jews until the Quarans and Falas Mora began to petition Israel for the right to immigrate. The Quarans came to Israel in 1999. Most of the Falas Mora remain in Ethiopia, emigrating to Israel annually in small numbers. The people of Israel continue to respond to the Falas Mora, allowing small numbers to emigrate annually.

16

A Mother's Quest

A Folktale from Scotland Retold

The calm blue water mirrored the fading azure sky as a lone fisherman guided his boat into the cove and headed toward home. Steering his skiff clear of the jagged rocks, he glanced upward at the charcoal gray cliffs and something strange caught his eye. He pulled the boat closer and glimpsed the dim outline of a body. "Have mercy on the poor soul," he exclaimed aloud and deftly guided the boat into the rocky shore. He scrambled up the cliff and found a young woman lying on a rock ledge. Her ginger-colored hair covered her upturned face; she lay motionless on her back, her right arm draped limply across her chest, her other stretched outward, her hand clutching a clod of grass and earth. The fisherman pulled back her hair, bent his ear to her lips and listened. She was still breathing. "Lass, I've got to get you home so the missus can take care of you," he whispered as he picked up her limp body and carried her to his boat.

When the fisherman's wife saw the blue cast of the woman's lips, she immediately put her to bed, covered her with extra blankets, and heaped more sticks on the fire. After a careful examination, she turned to her husband and said, "Poor thing, she had a terrible fall. She's bruised and dazed but nothing is broken." All through the night, the fisherman's wife watched over the frail young woman. As she kept vigil, she noticed the delicacy of the woman's features, her pale, almost transparent skin, and the way her auburn hair glinted like red gold in the firelight. Toward morning, the woman became restless, tossing her head back and forth and moaning softly. Her whimpers turned to cries and she sat bolt upright, calling out, "Where's my child, my wee baby boy?"

The fisherman's wife tried to calm her. "Hush now. It's all right. You've had a terrible fall but you're safe now."

The woman's blank face stared at the fisherman's wife and in an urgent whisper, she repeated her question. "Where's my child?"

"My dear lass, we found no child, only you. You tumbled over the bank," replied the fisherman's wife as she reached out to grab hold of the woman's hand.

"I needed water," said the woman, yanking her hand away. "I wrapped him up in his blanket and left him safely tucked under a bush between two rocks at the side of the path." She pulled back the blankets and pushed aside the sheets, frantically searching for her missing infant. "Where is he?" she screamed.

Awakened by the woman's cry, the fisherman came into the room. "What's the matter?" he asked.

"The lass had a babe with her," explained his wife. "She left him by the path. You must go look for him, he's been out alone all night!"

The fisherman gathered two of his neighbors and together they rowed out to the cliffs. All morning long, the men searched, examining every gorse bush and stone along the path, combing through the fields, but they found no trace of the child.

When the fisherman returned to his cottage, the woman was sitting in a chair next to the fire sipping a cup of tea. She turned her head as soon as he walked in the door and asked, "Did you find him?"

The fisherman shook his head. "I'm sorry. We looked and looked, but there's no sign of him. None at all," said the fisherman in a soft voice.

"A child just doesn't disappear. He must be somewhere. I've got to find him." She stood up and moved toward the door.

"You're too weak, my child," said the fisherman's wife. "Stay here till you are well, then you can go look for the child."

"You don't understand. His father died before he was born. Both my parents are dead and gone. I can't let another person slip out of my life. Besides, he needs me," she declared. The fisherman and his wife pleaded with the young woman, but she would not be deterred. She took the warm shawl and the food they offered, and left them with a promise. "You've been very kind to me. I'll come back as soon as I have found my babe."

The young woman walked through the countryside, in and out of the villages, knocking on every door she saw, stopping every passerby. Each time she asked the same question, a desperate appeal born of misery and edged with hope: "Have you seen my child, my sweet baby boy?" The answer did not change; no one had seen her child. She continued her frenzied search, stopping only for an occasional cup of tea or a few spoonfuls of soup, sleeping under bushes and in fields. As the days passed, her hope slowly trickled away.

One evening, the young woman made her way into the forest and came upon a clearing where a group of gypsies had set up camp. She huddled next to a tree watching them until a little girl noticed her. Tugging on her mother's skirt, she pointed to the young woman. When the girl's mother saw the weary, bedraggled stranger, she invited her to join them round the fire. The gypsies bathed the young woman's tired feet, then scooped a bowl of stew from the pot and handed it to her. Between bites, she told them of her lost child and her fruitless search to find him.

"We are heading north to join another camp," said one of the men. "There is an old grandmother there who is very wise and can see things the rest of us cannot understand. Perhaps she will be able to help you find your child." Encouraged by this possibility, the young woman followed the gypsies to the next camp.

When they arrived, the man brought her to a white-haired old crone who sat knitting by the fire. She looked up, revealing a tiny, brown face crinkled into soft furrows by the passage of time, and with a penetrating gaze carefully examined the young woman. The young woman noted that the old woman's eyes were different colors; one was deep blue, while the other was dark brown.

"You look as if you were carrying the weight of the world on those slender shoulders," the old woman remarked, putting away her knitting in a basket by her side. "Come, sit beside me and tell me what ails you." For the remainder of the day and late into the night, the two women sat together, the old woman nodding her whitened head from time to time, as she listened to the young woman release her sorrows. The young woman explained that her parents had died when she was only twelve and, as a result, she had learned to fend for herself. With a smile on her face, she recalled her marriage at sixteen to a handsome young farmer, and their joy when they found she was going to have a child. The fever claimed him just two weeks before their baby boy was born. "And now my boy's gone too," said the young woman. "Can you tell me his whereabouts?"

The old woman reached into her basket, drew forth a handful of dried herbs, and tossed them into the fire. Thick curls of gray smoke swirled upwards, filling the air with a pungent fragrance. The old woman leaned forward and with open hands fanned the haze toward her face. She breathed deeply. When the cloud of smoke dissolved, she spoke slowly. "Joy bound up with sorrow," she murmured. "Your child is alive but he has been stolen away by the fairies, the Sidh. They have taken him to their fairy rath, the Sidhean."

The young woman knew about the Sidh; they were powerful fairies who lived deep within the hollow hills. "Can't you help me?" asked the young woman.

"I understand the ways of nature," answered the kind crone, "but fairy magic is stronger than my knowledge."

"Please, you've got to do something," begged the young woman. "I have no other hope."

The old woman sighed. She looked into the young woman's eyes that, for the first time since she had met her, brimmed with tears. "Go to sleep, my child. I'll see what I can do." All night long, the old woman stared at the fire, poking the glowing embers with a stick and watching the glittering column of sparks dance into the coal-black sky.

In the morning, the old woman summoned the younger woman. "There may be something you can do after all. This is what I know.

The fairies are gathering in the Sidhean to select one of their own to rule over them for the next hundred years. From all across the land they will come. If you can enter into the Sidhean with some of them, you have a chance at getting back your babe."

"How can I enter the Sidhean?" asked the young woman. "And how will I get my baby out?"

"The key to it all is this," explained the gypsy grandmother. "The fairies have great magic but they have no skill when it comes to making things. Whatever objects they have, they must beg, steal, or borrow. They have an eye for fancy things and desire to possess articles of uncommon beauty or exceptional quality. You'll need one thing to buy your way into the Sidhean and another to get your baby back."

"Where can I find these things?" asked the young mother.

"That I do not know, but they must be things that are rare beyond comparison or one of a kind," said the old woman. Then the old crone carefully explained how to find the entrance to the Sidhean. "Right now the veils between the two worlds are very thin. The best time to see the fairies is just when the light of day is fading and becoming night." Reaching into her basket, she took out a small jar and handed it the young mother. "Take this ointment and rub it on your eyelids. It will help you see the fairies."

The young woman sat silently, trying to take in all that she had just heard. The old woman slowly got up and straightened her bent back. She placed her knotted hands on top of the young woman's head and, with an ancient charm, asked the earth, air, fire, and water to keep her safe from harm. "For one so young, you have overcome many troubles," she declared. "You will need that strength for the task ahead."

The gypsies broke camp, and the young woman remained in the forest. She wove her way through the snarl of trees, trying to unscramble the tangle of thoughts in her head. She recalled the stories of her childhood and tried to remember all the wondrous objects contained in those tales. Two things stuck out, articles that filled everyone with awe—the white cloak of Nechtan, whose holy well was a source of great knowledge, and the golden-stringed harp of an ancient blind bard. With each footstep, her thoughts became clearer and a plan took shape in her mind.

The young woman left the woods and made her way back toward the sea, where she found shelter in a tiny cave by the water's edge. Every day she ascended the steep rocks lining the pebbled shore, searching the cracks and crevices for the downy fluff from the birds that nested there. Not once did the wind blow the tiny feathers out of her reach. The waves never washed over her with the rising tide. She did not cut her feet along the rocks, and the sun did not beat down upon her back. Such was the power of the old woman's words that the elements protected her.

When the young woman had collected enough tiny feathers to form two huge puffs at the back of the cave, she took a knife and cut off her auburn hair. It lay in a golden russet heap next to the white down. She began to weave the silky feathers and the strands of her hair together in an exquisite pattern until she had formed a downy cloak so light to the touch that one could not feel its weight upon the shoulders. It fluttered in the slightest breeze and shimmered in the sunlight like a thousand tiny stars. She folded it with great care, placed it atop a stone slab inside the cave, and set a driftwood branch on top to keep it from floating away.

The young woman then began to search the shoreline for material to make the frame of a harp. She came upon the skeletal remains of a large seal poking out of a cleft in the rocks. The sun-bleached bones had been polished as smooth as ivory by the rocking motion of the shifting tides. The young woman dragged the skeleton out of the fissure and used a rock to pry loose an expanse of ribs that she molded into a frame. With the remaining strands of her cut hair, she strung the harp and tuned it to the rhythm of the sea. When she played her music, the gulls of the air ceased their shrieking and came to rest on the sand to listen.

All the while the young woman worked, she kept her mind on her task, pushing thoughts of her missing baby into the shadowy recesses of her mind, keeping her grief hidden so that it would not overwhelm hope. When the cloak and harp were completed, the pangs of longing seized her. She took her creations, fled the shelter of the cave, and walked through the fields and forests, stopping only long enough to drink from the brooks and streams. After three days, she arrived at a wide grassy plain that swelled into a verdant knoll. Recalling the gypsy grandmother's instructions, she searched the grass until she found the three circles of clearer green that marked the entrance to the fairy rath, the Sidhean. She hid herself in a thicket of gorse, smeared her eyelids with the old woman's ointment, and waited.

As the light of day faded, the young woman saw fairies troop by in bunches and disappear into the mound. The creatures moved with airy grace, their slender bodies glistening gold, copper, and bronze, radiant with an inner light. Finally, a lone fairy woman appeared and the lass saw her chance to enter the hollow hill. She draped the cloak over her shoulders and moved out from behind the bush. When the fairy woman saw her, she hissed, "What is the likes of you doing here? This is no place for human folk. Go on, get out of here!" and she took a step forward. The cape of feathers quivered. The fairy stopped and stared. The young woman twirled slightly one way then another, and the cloak wafted up into the air, a swirling cloud of down. The fairy woman's garnet eyes widened and she reached out her shiny copper hand to stroke the downy softness. When she did, the cloak glittered in response. "Woman, what will you take for that cape?" she asked.

"This cloak is not for sale," declared the young woman. She lifted it by the edge and brushed the cape lightly across the fairy's outstretched arm, sending a shiver of delight through her coppery body.

"I'll shower you with gold. Give me that cape," implored the fairy.

"I do not want your gold," said the young woman, "but there is something you can give me in exchange." The fairy leaned closer. "Take me into the Sidhean," she whispered.

The fairy woman smiled and reached out her hands to grab her trophy. "Give me the cape."

The young woman knew that fairies were a treacherous folk, unconcerned with the laws of honor. "Take me in first," she demanded. The fairy woman extended her burnished palm and she placed her fingers on top. For a moment, the fairy and the woman were engulfed in a haze of tiny jewel-like sparks, and then a door appeared. The fairy and the young woman entered and the door closed behind them.

When the fairies saw a mortal woman in their midst, they clustered round her, ready to fling her out of the rath. She quickly slipped the cloak from her shoulders and made a great show of placing the mantle on the fairy woman. As they watched the trembling feathers drape over the fairy woman's shoulder like a giant wing, they began to argue and plead, each vying for a chance to wear and feel the delicate cloak. The young lass walked away without being noticed as the fairies' brittle exclamations of admiration and envy jangled in the air.

The young woman strode through the hall until she came upon the newly crowned fairy king sitting on his gold and diamond throne. Boldly, she walked toward the throne, her harp in her hands. The silver-skinned king cocked his head to one side and remarked, "Well, what have we here? A mortal woman and a harp?"

The young woman strummed the strings in a decisive thrum resembling thunder. The king's interest was piqued. "Play some more," he said, and she began to play a tune so captivating that the king was unable to take his eyes off the harp of bone. In the middle of the riff, she stopped. "Give me that harp!" demanded the king.

"No, not for all the world. It is mine." The young lass stroked the strings of hair, letting the sorrow she carried in her heart seep through her fingers. The mournful melody filled the hall with such intensity that the fairies stopped arguing and gathered round.

"I'll trade you gold for the harp," cried the king. He had gold piled so high that it reached the lass's ankles.

"No," she declared, never even glancing at the glittering heaps. "Give me my baby boy, the child your fairies have stolen away."

The king was reluctant; a mortal babe was an uncommon treasure and he wanted the child for himself. She continued to play, the music giving shape to her yearning. The fairies stood as still as statues; even the fairy king leaned forward on his throne. He had jewels of every kind carried in and mounded so deep they reached her waist. "No one in your world has a fortune such as this," he bellowed.

"Give me my child," she groaned. She grasped hold of the harp with a fierce determination and played a tune of reckoning so powerful that the walls of the Sidhean sighed with regret. The fairy king had the child brought out. When the lass saw him, a cry escaped her throat, but she held the harp firm until they placed the babe in the crook of her arm. Then she let go of the harp and kissed her child, bringing his soft cheek next to hers.

The harp slid down the jeweled pile onto the floor, where it landed at the king's feet. He reached down, clutched the bone frame, and started to play the wild and haunting music of the fairy realm.

The young mother turned away and left the Sidhean, the fairy music no match for the peace and joy she felt as she cradled her child in her arms. Outside, a full moon hung in the night sky, its pale light turning the grassy field into a silver plain. The young woman carried her baby through the countryside down to the fisherman's little cottage by the cove. In the early morning light, she knocked on the door and the fisherman and his wife welcomed her with much delight. The young woman raised her son by the sea, and together they lived happily in that village surrounded by the love of good friends for many years.

The hero's quest is a common motif in folktales and mythology, retold in countless variations. Often the hero is wrenched out of the familiar or abandoned in a dark place and must overcome tremendous obstacles to regain a lost love or obtain a rare treasure. The search is treacherous and the hero frequently must visit strange worlds, but along the way, the hero encounters ordinary friends and magical creatures that provide companionship, assistance, and good advice. In many tales, the hero is an ordinary person who develops strength, competence, and wisdom from the experiences of the journey. When the tasks

are accomplished and the prize gained, the transformed hero returns to the place of origin or abandonment to live a new life.

The hero's quest is a recognizable pattern of self-discovery and can help us understand how our lives work. We face many trials in our life—loneliness, betrayal, loss of health, death, the capriciousness of fate. Damaged and weakened, we enter into the darkness of our troubles and struggle through the difficult times. We try to make sense out of what has happened and search for guidance. We look outward and accept the help of friends, wise counselors, teachers, holy men and women. We look inward and discover unknown resources and strength, blessings of spirit. We emerge from our time of trial, healed and restored, with newfound capabilities that enable us to continue on our journeys of transformation.

17

The Miser

An Aesop Fable Retold

There was once a lackluster little man who trudged through his monotonous days without enthusiasm. His parents were dead and he lived in the shadow of their former life, occupying their gloomy house and running his father's tedious business. His only companions were a disinterested housekeeper, a worried cook, and a few thieving mice.

One day, on his way to work, he saw something sparkling in the bushes. Bending down, he parted the leaves and found a gold coin glinting in the sunlight. He picked it up and immediately put it in his pocket so that no one else would see it. When he returned home that evening, he buried the coin underneath the socks in his top bureau drawer. After the servants went to bed, he retrieved the coin and, holding it under the subdued lamplight, watched it shimmer in his open palm. He rubbed it between his fingers, feeling its easy smoothness, its solid mass, and reveled in the fact that it belonged to him and no one else. The little man began to look forward to his nightly ritual when he would withdraw to his room, lock his door, and spend time admiring the golden purity of his solitary coin.

After a time, one coin no longer satisfied his craving; he hungered for more. He sold the silent piano in the living room, along with the overstuffed velvet chairs. He stripped the walls of their paintings and brought them to an art dealer. Soon, the miser amassed more gold coins than his bureau drawer could safely hold. Tucked away in the dusty clutter of the attic, he found an empty chest with a padlock and dragged it down the stairs to his room. He poured the contents of the drawer into the bottom of the box and shoved it under his bed. His nights were spent counting the number of coins in the chest and stacking them into glittering, golden piles.

However, the empty space inside the box troubled the miser, and he sought to fill it. One by one, all the fine things in the house disappeared. The stingy little man carted his mother's jewelry off to the pawnshop, loaded up a wagon with her china and crystal, and traded everything for more gold. He dismissed the housekeeper, and the cook left because she tired of trying to make meals out of poor cuts of meat and vegetables discarded by the grocer. None of it mattered to the miser. The only thing that interested him was the box of coins hidden underneath his bed. He stayed awake until the wee hours of the morning, kneeling beside the chest, lifting handfuls of gold out of the gleaming heap, and listening to the delicate chink and tinkle as the coins cascaded back into the box.

Late one night, a thief skulking through the darkness saw the golden light coming from the miser's window. Tiptoeing up to the window, he peered inside and saw the little man bent over the chest of gold. The next day, while the miser was at work, the thief snuck into the house and emptied the chest of its golden hoard. He filled seven bags with coins, hauled them out the back door, hid them underneath some rags in a cart, and drove away, disguised as a peddler. No one saw a thing.

When the miserly man returned home, he went directly to his room to check on his gold. In the middle of the floor, with its lid flung wide open, sat the barren chest, bereft of its treasure. The miser bent down and put his hand in the box, frantically feeling around for a stray coin or two. "No, no, it can't be," he muttered to himself.

He looked under the bed and yanked open every drawer in his bureau, hoping to find a trace of his missing gold. Finally, the miser realized that it was gone. He threw back his head, raised his fists into the air, and shrieked, "No! No! No!" His distressing howls penetrated the closed doors and windows, alarming a nearby neighbor who came running. The neighbor pushed open the back door and made his way through the dim, dusty hallway, following the sound of the miser's screaming.

"What is the matter?" he called out to the frenzied miser as he entered the bedroom.

"It's gone. All of it," moaned the miser.

"What is gone?" asked the neighbor.

"My gold. Someone has taken all my gold!"

The neighbor stared at the wilted figure in front of him. With his tattered coat, frayed trousers, and worn-out boots, the miser looked more like a scarecrow than a man. The neighbor scrutinized the shabby room, his keen gaze taking in the threadbare blanket, the peeling wallpaper, the cold fireplace devoid of logs, and the cobwebs hanging from unadorned windows.

"You had gold?" he exclaimed.

"Yes, in that chest," declared the miser. "It was full of golden coins."

"Didn't you ever use them?" asked the neighbor in surprise.

The miser shook his head. Amazed, the neighbor continued, "You never bought a coat to keep you warm, never bothered to buy wood for a fire, never thought to purchase a thick blanket to cover you up at night?"

"No, I only looked at the coins," said the miser.

"You never used the money at all—not once?" asked the neighbor.

"No, I never used it. I just looked at it," repeated the miser.

"Then come and look into the empty chest," said the neighbor. "It will do you just as much good." The neighbor walked out of the freezing-cold house, shaking his head, while the miser stared into the blank hole that was his chest of gold.

The miser responds to the world around him with fear-filled anxiety, accumulating wealth in an effort to assuage his feelings of uneasiness. It is not an uncommon response. We hold fast to what we know and we become defensive, unwilling to change our attitudes or accept new ways of doing things because we are frightened by the shifting relationships in our families, our neighborhoods, and our nations. We seek financial investments that can safeguard us against natural disasters and capricious twists of fortune. We even hide our talents, worried that others will not fully appreciate our abilities or that using our skills will exhaust us. We sense that things are out of control and are afraid to trust in anything beyond ourselves. However, if we can let go of some of our fears, we recognize the goodness that resides in people and in the world around us. If we learn to appreciate that goodness, we are able to respond with gratitude rather than fear.

18

Mary McPhee and the Pooka

An Irish Tale Retold

Mary McPhee lived in a tiny stone house in a remote part of the country with nothing but her cat and her memories to keep her company. Her parents had died many years before, and she remained in that little cabin, following a routine that had not changed since she was a girl. Lonesomeness was a familiar part of her life, and she put it in its proper place with the thought, "There's plenty who are worse off than the likes of me." She blessed the sun when it shone and praised the rain for making the grass grow. In her heart, Mary kept alive a flicker of hope that something wonderful was waiting for her just around the corner. It might take awhile to find, but she was convinced that it was there; it was just a matter of looking in the right place.

Mary seldom had two coins to rub together. She ran errands and did extra chores for nearby farmwives, occasionally receiving a penny or two for her labors. More often than not, she simply earned a plate of cabbage and boiled potatoes or a slice of buttered bread and a cup of tea. She made do and was grateful for the food and whatever else might come her way.

One day, a young boy appeared at Mary's door with a plea for help. His youngest brother and sister were sick with the croup and his mother needed help with the washing and cooking of the meals. "Will you come, Mary McPhee?" he asked in a solemn voice.

"Of course I will," she answered, reaching up to grab her shawl from the peg by the door.

It had been a long, troubled walk for the child and as they returned to his home, he revealed his worries to Mary. "Mary, are you not afraid walking this lonely stretch of road at night by yourself?"

"Afraid? No, I've walked this road all my life. What is there to be frightened of?" Mary replied.

"Why, Mary McPhee, surely you've heard of the pooka. He travels these roads at night, playing tricks on folks and causing all sorts of devilment."

"Oh, that old black horse—he's nothing to be afraid of. His tricks are harmless. All he does is turn himself into a pile of straw that can't be lifted or spoil the berries or bewitch a cow and get it to kick over a milk pail. Why would I be afraid of nonsense like that?"

"Mary McPhee, have you not heard the other stories? How he knocks people into ditches, scares them with his fiery blue eyes, bruises them with his great big hooves, and takes them away on wild night rides!"

"Ah, he only abuses them that's afraid of him. I'm not a bit afraid. In fact, I'd welcome a ride through the countryside. It would be a grand adventure the likes of which I've never had!"

"Oh, Mary, don't say such things. You never know who is listening," cautioned the boy. When Mary heard the child's innocent reproach, she gave a hoot and the sound of her laughter tinkled across the fields and up into the air.

Mary spent the remainder of the day working. She washed the clothes, hung them on the line, and, as they dried, she started the stew simmering and baked the bread. After she served the other children their supper, Mary cleaned up the dishes and brought in the clothes as the sun sidled its way out of the reddened sky. The woman finally tucked her children into bed for the night, then sat down with Mary to enjoy a welcome bowl of mutton stew. As the two women ate their meal, Mary felt weariness creep into her worn body. She sipped the last of her tea, wrapped her shawl around her shoulders, and bade the woman good-night. "Will you be all right, Mary?" asked the woman. "It's late and it's a long walk back to your place."

"Don't worry about me," said Mary. "There's a full moon out to light my path. I'll be just fine." Mary moseyed along, feeling the weight of her tired feet and enjoying the peacefulness of the evening. The moon cast a silvery sheen over the landscape and caused lacy shadows to fall across the fields. "Just lovely," muttered Mary to herself, and then she stumbled over something in the road. Looking down, Mary saw an old, black pot. "Well now, that's an odd thing to find abandoned in the middle of the road," she remarked. "But you never know, it might come in handy. I'll just take it along with me and see what comes of it."

She bent down to lift the pot by its handle and saw that it was filled with gold coins. "Goodness gracious," she exclaimed, standing bolt upright in shock. She circled the pot several times, observing it from all angles to make sure that it was real and when it didn't disappear, she thought to herself, "It would be foolish to leave it here. Why, it's just sitting here, waiting for me to take it home." However, the pot was too heavy to carry, so Mary tied her shawl around it and began to drag it down the road.

As Mary lugged the pot behind her, she imagined the things she could do with her newfound riches, her ruminations moving from the practical to the fantastic, until she chuckled to herself and muttered, "Mary McPhee, you're putting on airs. What would the likes of you be doing in a castle with servants?"

After a while, Mary had to stop and catch her breath because hauling the pot was hard work. Turning around, she gave a cry of surprise for she discovered that her pot of gold had turned into a huge lump of shining silver. "Well, will you look at that!" she exclaimed. "It is indeed a strange night. A lump of silver may not be a pot of gold, but it's more convenient and easier to keep safe." She adjusted the shawl, took a deep breath, and continued down the road, pulling the treasure behind her.

The lump of silver weighed almost as much as the pot of gold, and soon Mary had to stop again to rest. She turned around and this time saw that the lump of silver had become a great lump of iron. "The moonlight must be playing tricks on my poor, tired eyes. Nevertheless, a lump of iron is more than I had when I woke up this morning." With a smile on her face, she took hold of the shawl and made her way back to her cottage.

When Mary got home, she reached down to pick up the lump of iron and, in the moonlight, saw that it had become an ordinary stone. With a laugh, she declared, "Luck has been with me this whole night. The lump of iron is nothing more than a stone, but isn't that exactly what I need to prop open my front door."

Mary untied the shawl, lifted it off the stone, and wrapped it around her shoulders. The stone began to shiver and shake and Mary watched in amazement as it bounced and jumped about, sprouting four legs, a long neck, and a tail, until it became a fine black horse with eyes the color of blue flames. It switched its silken tail, shook its powerful head, and pawed the ground with its mighty front hoof. "That pot of gold befuddled my brains," said Mary, shaking her head. "I should have known that such peculiar antics were the workings of none other than the pooka himself!"

The pooka bent its head until its fiery eyes were level with Mary's face. In a gravelly human voice it asked, "Would you like to go for a ride, Mary McPhee?"

Without hesitation, Mary replied, "Indeed, I would." The horse bent its neck and Mary hitched up her skirt, grabbed hold of the horse's long mane, and pulled herself onto its back. The pooka gave a mighty leap and sprang into the air. They raced along, the pooka's hooves barely touching the earth as they bounded across the fields and flew over the hills. The pins that held Mary's hair bound came loose and her long tresses streamed out behind her. "Look at me," she hollered out with glee. "I'm flying!"

The pooka came to an abrupt halt at a spot where two roads crossed and stomped the ground with its hoof. All of a sudden, a thin gray cloud of mist began to float over the surrounding fields. It glimmered in the moonlight, swirling higher and closer, thickening as it twirled, until it was so dense that Mary could not see her own hand in front of her face. Then slowly, the silvery haze faded away and revealed a fine, big house with a delicate blue light spilling out of its open door. "Go on in, Mary McPhee," said the horse, bowing its head to the ground. Mary slipped off the pooka's back and made a quick attempt to straighten her disheveled hair and clothes. Warily, she stepped into the patch of light, placed her hand on the doorframe, and peered inside.

Mary's eyes widened in astonishment as she gazed at the spectacle arrayed before her. Hundreds of blue-white flames hovered in the air, casting a pearly sheen over the most beautiful people Mary had ever seen. Their dazzling blue eyes twinkled as they chattered and laughed, the sound of their voices rippling through the room like a spring rain. Every one of them had white hair and alabaster skin, but none wore the signs of age. Music drifted up from the earth below, a delicate, haunting melody that silenced the conversation. As Mary stood in the doorway, the people began to dance, moving around the room with the fragile agility of moths fluttering through the night.

A man wearing a waistcoat of dove-gray feathers walked toward Mary and extended an elegant hand. "Would you care to dance, Mary McPhee?" he asked. Mary nodded her head and placed her work-worn fingers in his translucent palm. She seemed to float across the floor as he led her to the center of the room. All traces of fatigue departed from Mary's body as she danced like a feather on the wind, allowing the music to seep into her bones and carry her around the room. Mary danced all night long. Outside, morning approached through the open door and in the face of its soft light, the blue-white flames weakened. The alabaster people slowly dissolved, the edges of their bodies blurring until they completely vanished from sight. The music wafted away and Mary found herself standing in the middle of an empty field as dawn brightened the horizon.

The pooka stood next to her and in a hoarse whisper gently announced, "I think it's time to go home, Mary McPhee." With a few powerful strides, the pooka carried Mary back to her humble cottage and deposited her next to her front door.

"Good-night, Mary McPhee," said the pooka.

"Thank you," answered Mary. "It has been a grand evening."

"Indeed, it has," declared the pooka. "Now you've got a story to tell, Mary McPhee, and you can remind your neighbors that the pooka is more than tricks and treachery." The pooka kicked up his heels, gave a loud whinny, and galloped down the road. Mary watched until the great black horse was just a speck in the distance, then she went inside.

Mary put on the kettle and brewed herself a cup of strong tea. She sat in her chair, sipping her tea and related the night's adventures to her ginger-colored cat curled up on her lap. "Oh, puss," she said, "it was a night of wonders. I will remember it all my born days. I would never trade it for anything, not for a lump of iron, or a hunk of shining silver, not even for a pot full of golden coins."

An old Scottish proverb says, "Were it not for hope, the heart would break." An attitude of hopefulness can allow us to respond openly to the possibilities that life offers. Hope entails clear vision; we are conscious of the problems in the world and see the obstacles in our daily lives. We do not blithely suppose that all will be well. In times of hardship, we look backward at our collective history, examine our spirituality, listen to the stories of our ancestors, and see that we can triumph over difficulty. The memory of the past offers a promise for the future and we are able to declare our confidence in the goodness of this world.

This recognition of the underlying goodness of things helps us view others sympathetically and enables us to be open to the world around us. Hope encourages us to see things differently and imagine creative solutions to our problems. We are willing to set aside our fears, take risks, and work to bring about changes in our environment.

According to a common version of the Greek myth of Pandora, she ignores Zeus's interdiction and opens a box, letting loose all the trials and tribulations of this world. Pandora tries to undo her mistake and close the lid, but the troubles have escaped. All that remains is hope. However, there is another version of this story. Instead of evils, the box contains Pandora's marriage blessings. When she unfastens the latch, the blessings float out into the world and Pandora is unable to retrieve them. Hope is left at the bottom of the box, because it is hope that makes us reach for the good that is in the world, even when it seems to be beyond our grasp.

19

This Too Shall Pass

A Folktale from Iran Retold

The ruler of Nishabur stepped out onto his terrace as the delicate blush of the morning sun began to warm the sky. "What a wonderful day!" he exclaimed. Sitting down to breakfast, he smiled at his servant and said, "Look, the sun has risen just to greet me." The servant smiled back woodenly, nodded his head, and returned to the kitchen.

"His Honor is in fine form today!" he commented to the cook.

"It won't last long," the cook replied. "Yesterday morning he said that my sweet rolls were heavenly delights and I was an exquisite cook. At dinner, he complained that the soup was cold and told me I wasn't fit to serve a meal to the dogs. His moods are like the wind— first they blow this way and then they blow that way." The cook waved his hand through the air with a sweeping motion. The two men shook their heads and sighed. The ruler of Nishabur was a tiresome man, whose impetuous behavior made life difficult for everyone within the palace walls.

The twelve advisors stood ceremoniously and bowed their heads when the ruler of Nishabur entered the council chambers. After exchanging the customary greetings, one by one they began to deliver their reports regarding the state of affairs in the kingdom. The first to speak was the minister of agriculture, a plump, unctuous fel-

low who wore a robe made of the finest silk. He smirked ingratiat-
ingly and peppered his remarks with compliments directed toward
the ruler. "As Your Honor can plainly see, being a man of great intelligence and keen understanding, my plans are timely and efficient,"
declared the minister as he finished.

"Well done," said the ruler of Nishabur.

The minister of finance gave a slight cough. Several other advisors
presented information weaving sweet talk and smiles in with their
comments. Each one received a nod of approval from the ruler of
Nishabur. The minister of finance gave no sign of encouragement to
the men. Instead, his eyes widened and his eyebrows arched until,
finally, he stood up decisively and in a stern voice asserted, "Your
Honor, the ideas set forth here are costly and unwise. I beg you to
consider these proposals more carefully." The minister of finance
clearly stated his objections, supporting them with a neat array of facts.

As the ruler of Nishabur listened, he realized that the minister's
arguments made sense, but the man's straightforward manner and
razor-sharp voice grated on his nerves. His good humor quickly dissolved into petulance. He allowed the minister to continue for a
while, then interrupted him curtly, saying, "You have made your
point. Let us stop, refresh ourselves with some food, and digest your
comments." They retired to the dining room, where the ruler of
Nishabur pouted throughout the meal.

As he walked through the corridor on his way back to the council chamber, the ruler passed an open courtyard where he saw two of
his advisors. The two men sat next to each other on a bench with
their backs toward the ruler, their heads bent in earnest conversation.
Hoping to escape notice, the ruler furtively stepped behind a column
to listen.

"Well, I wonder if we can cajole our ruler into a good mood for
the afternoon. In his present frame of mind, he'll just sulk for the
remainder of the day, and he'll never listen to anything we have to
say," said one of the men.

"I am so weary of his unpredictability. He is so easily influenced by
his feelings that he doesn't stop to think beyond the present moment,"

replied the other. "I find more wisdom in my barbershop than I do in the council chambers." They both laughed with wry humor.

The words struck the ruler with the force of a punch in the stomach. That afternoon, as he tried to listen to the remaining reports of his advisors, the conversation he overheard echoed in his mind. His gaze shifted from one advisor to another, and, for the first time, he noticed their artificial grins and insincere flattery. Slowly, the ruler of Nishabur grasped the truth of what he had heard.

That evening, the ruler paced the floor of his bedchamber, pondering his own shortcomings. Memories of past foolishness kept darting in and out of his mind, causing him to cringe with embarrassment. However, when he looked beyond his errors in judgment, he found something else hiding beneath his discomfiture—a longing to be an honest, wise, and generous ruler. "Why," he thought to himself, "can't I be the sort of ruler I want to be? I want to be good and kind, but my foolishness gets in the way every time." He stood in the middle of his floor and, addressing the empty room, cried out, "What is wrong with me?"

Thinking that perhaps a medical condition was causing his problem, the ruler summoned his physician. The doctor thoroughly examined him, checking his heart, his eyes, and his ears, and observing his reflexes. "You are in perfect health," he announced.

"That can't be," bellowed the ruler. "Something is wrong with me and you have to fix it!"

"Your problem lies not with your physical health, but with your spiritual character," said the doctor. "You need a guiding principle that will force you to stop and think, so you can achieve balance and peace of mind. Have you read the great philosophers of the past and the celebrated thinkers of our times?"

The ruler's face crinkled with confusion. "No, no … I haven't."

"Well, I suggest that you start there. Wisdom isn't gained overnight," said the doctor as he packed up his instruments.

The ruler wanted to argue with his physician, but something in his better nature forced him to stop. "You are right," he said. "I have been shortsighted. It is time to move to a deeper level of thinking."

In the morning, the ruler sent for an imam—a Muslim cleric—and a scholar. He explained his problem to them. "I need guidance. I need to learn how to pause and reflect so that I am not overwhelmed by my emotions."

"Your Honor," said the imam, "you need to enlarge your perspective. Look at the entire breadth of life. Go to the graveyard and sit for a while amid the tombs. Your rashness will be tempered when you realize that nothing, including you, will last forever."

The ruler considered the imam's advice. "No, no, that won't do," he said. "How can I rule the country if I run off to the graveyard every time I need to think? I need something that I can always keep with me, something that will point me in the right direction."

It was the scholar's turn to speak. "Assemble a group of learned men and listen to their counsel."

"I already have a circle of advisors."

"I mean no disrespect, Your Honor," said the scholar, "but you have surrounded yourself with many who are fools and flatterers. You need to find wise and sincere councillors, honest men who possess good judgment. They will keep you from acting unwisely."

The ruler replied, "It is a worthy idea, but I don't think it will work. It will take too long. I cannot govern effectively if I have to wait for an entire circle of people to agree before I make a decision." The ruler sighed and stared at the floor for several minutes and then spoke in a soft voice. "Please understand. I know the difference between right and wrong. It's just that when I am flattered, I let my pride get in the way. And if things don't work out the way I want them to, I get angry. No one has faith in my judgment. How can they? I'm as changeable as the wind." His gaze shifted and he looked directly at the imam and the scholar. "I need to be able to make my own decisions. I need a simple directive that offers me guidance in every situation."

"It is a good idea," declared the scholar. "This city is filled with great thinkers. Call them together and tell them that you are in need of a straightforward maxim that sheds light on every circumstance."

The ruler of Nishabur sent out a proclamation, and the next week the great conference commenced. Philosophers, theologians, poets, artists, scholars, and imams all crowded together in the great hall. At first, things proceeded in an orderly fashion. Poems were recited, songs were sung, and sermons preached, all in an effort to provide the ruler of Nishabur with the necessary bit of wisdom. He listened carefully, but nothing was satisfactory. "Too long. Too complicated. I'll never remember that," he commented as various suggestions were presented. The intellectuals consulted ancient texts and modern treatises looking for suitable instructions. They began to bicker back and forth, each person clamoring to be heard, until the din of their raucous voices filled the room. "None of this makes any sense!" shouted the ruler, and he stormed out of the hall.

He made his way into the garden and settled himself on a bench underneath a black mulberry tree. As the ruler breathed in the fragrant air and took in the pleasant atmosphere, his anxiety lessened. Nearby, one of the gardeners was tugging weeds out of the soil and throwing them into a pile. The old man observed the ruler and, after a few minutes, walked toward him. Bowing low, he addressed the ruler: "Excuse me, Your Honor, we seldom have the privilege of your presence in the garden. Is something troubling you?"

The ruler looked at the gardener. The old man carried the signs of long years of work in the open air. His face was brown and wrinkled, and dirt permanently rested under the fingernails of his weathered hands. The gardener leaned forward, tilting his head to one side. "Can I help?"

Relieved by the old man's hospitable demeanor, the ruler of Nishabur unburdened himself of his immediate concerns. "I have gathered together the most learned men of this city and asked them to provide a simple phrase that will direct me in all situations. I have listened to them for several days now and I have heard nothing that will help me."

"I see," murmured the gardener. He paused for a few minutes before speaking. "When I was a much younger man," he said, "I worked for a wealthy landowner who had many cattle. He was a kind and generous man who always treated me fairly. I complimented him by saying, 'You are lucky that you are so well off.' He smiled and said,

'Things can easily change. This too shall pass.' I was puzzled by his words. In a year's time, a flood raged through the village and destroyed my employer's farm. He and his family went to work for another property owner whose land was untouched by the flood. One day, I saw my former employer, dressed in rags, working in the fields. I went over to him and said, 'I am sorry for your family's misfortune.' He smiled and said, 'Remember, things change. This too shall pass.' Two years later, the wealthy property owner died. He had no heirs and left all of his property to the man who was my former employer. He lived out the rest of his life as a wealthy man. When he died, those words, *This too shall pass*, were written on his tombstone. I have carried the wisdom of those words with me ever since." The gardener bowed low once more and then, taking leave of the ruler, said, "If Your Honor pleases, I should get back to my chores."

The ruler nodded his head and said, "Thank you for your story. It has been very helpful." As the gardener continued his tasks, the ruler pondered his words until the afternoon sunlight began to fade. Then he stood up abruptly and hurried back to his palace.

The squabbling was still in full force when the ruler returned to the great hall. He stood before the assembly, raised his hands, and called for silence. "Listen, one and all, I have found a motto. It is quite simple really, just four words."

The great thinkers scoffed at the idea and murmured among themselves, "Four words—how can wisdom be distilled into four words?"

Over their whispered objections, the ruler stated the words clearly, so that everyone could hear. "*This too shall pass*. These words will guard my pride and keep my temper in check. They will help me reflect in every situation." Slowly he repeated the words, "This too shall pass."

Chaos erupted in the room. "That's absurd," exclaimed a scholar. "It lacks depth. It is ridiculously simplistic."

"It doesn't show right from wrong," cried another academic.

The ruler stood quietly and allowed the words to sink in. The turmoil dissolved into thoughtful mutterings as the thinkers mulled over the phrase. The ruler turned to an assistant and said, "Go tell the cook to prepare a festive dinner. I think we have something to celebrate." With a slight chuckle, the ruler turned and left the room.

The ruler of Nishabur had the words *This too shall pass* inscribed on a gold ring, which he placed on the third finger of his right hand and wore as a permanent reminder. When he felt the tide of emotion rise within him, he looked at the ring. When he needed to decide an important issue, he held the ring before his eyes. In time, he became known throughout the land as a wise and just ruler who was able to accept the good with the bad, ease sorrow by remembering joy, and find what was valuable in every circumstance that life offered.

This tale is based on a story written by the great Persian poet and mystic Farid al-Din, known as Attar, who was born in the twelfth century in a town near Nishabur in modern-day Iran. Attar wrote several volumes of poetry and prose, including The Conference of the Birds *about Sufi saints and* The Book of the Divine, *which contains a version of this story.*

There also exists a similar tale about King Solomon. In that story, King Solomon asks his minister for a ring that will make him happy when he is sad and sad when he is happy. After searching for many months, the advisor finds the ring in a tiny shop where a young jeweler, upon the advice of his elderly grandfather, inscribes onto the ring the Hebrew words Gam ze yaavor— *"This too shall pass."*

The only constant in our lives is change. Youth fades and old age nips at our heels. Fortunes shift and elation becomes bitter disappointment. Everything passes away with time; this is the transient nature of reality. We are often overcome by the immediate feelings of a situation, seeking to hold onto moments of happiness and wishing times of sadness would disappear quickly. However, when we reflect on what has happened in our lives, we begin to see how our experiences, the difficult as well as the rewarding ones, have given us valuable clues to the meaning of life. Oftentimes, the most painful experiences prompt us to change and allow us to reach deeper levels of under-standing and intimacy.

Sorrow and happiness exist together, one balancing the other in the changing flow of life. If we accept this inevitable reality, then we can learn the significance of the phrase This too shall pass. *Remembered joy will ease our sadness and the awareness of sorrow can be a potent reminder to celebrate life to the fullest.*

A Neighbor's Wisdom

Tales from India and China Retold

*M*ichael edged his old Volvo station wagon into the narrow driveway, barely missing the basketball hoop, parked the car in front of the empty garage, and slowly pushed open the door. It was 11:00 in the morning and the neighborhood was quiet, most of the men and women off at work, the children all in school. Michael undid his tie, slid it out of his button-down collar, unfastened his top shirt button, and sat down on his front porch steps, the tie dangling from his hand. He stared out at the well-kept yards with neatly trimmed bushes and well-maintained houses. The hushed orderliness of the place seemed strange and forlorn to him.

Michael heard footsteps and turned to see his neighbor Wei Lun coming up the sidewalk from around the bend. The old man had retired from his business several years before, and spent his days tending the small garden behind his house and puttering in the garage that he had converted into a woodworking shop. When Wei Lun saw Michael, he called out in a friendly voice, "You're home early."

"Yeah, not exactly by choice," replied Michael.

The old man came closer. "What happened?"

"Awhile back I mentioned to you that our company wasn't meeting its projected quarterly revenues," said Michael. "Well, management's solution to the problem was to let a few of us go. I don't have a job anymore."

"I'm sorry to hear that," said Wei.

"I haven't told Judy yet. Things are going to be kind of rough around here until I find a new job. Judy doesn't make enough money to support our family."

The old man remained silent in order to give Michael a space to express his frustrations.

"They treat us like we are nothing more than numbers on a balance sheet, like we aren't even human. It's just so damned unfair," Michael groaned.

"Time will tell," said Wei. "You never know what can happen."

He could see by the expression on Michael's face that this response was not expected. "Mind if I sit down?" he asked, gesturing toward the porch steps.

"Go ahead," replied Michael.

Wei Lun took a seat next to his neighbor and leaned forward, resting his elbows on his knees. "When I was a young boy," he said, "my father owned a beautiful chestnut stallion. It was too spirited for me to ride, but my older brother was strong enough to handle the horse. Everyone in the village admired that horse. One day, the horse jumped the fence and ran off. Our neighbors came to my father and expressed their sadness over his loss. He smiled and said, 'Time will tell. You never know what can happen.' Two days later, the stallion returned with two wild piebald mares. Our neighbors congratulated my father on his luck. 'Time will tell. You never know what can happen,' he said, shrugging his shoulders. My brother tried to break one of the mares, so that he could saddle the horse and ride her. Unfortunately, the horse trampled him and he broke his leg very badly and was bedridden for several weeks. Again, the neighbors came to my father and offered their sympathy for my brother's condition. My father gave his usual response, 'Time will tell. You never know what can happen.' Now, as you know, I grew up in a country far away. Things were different. Two weeks after my brother broke his leg, officials from the army came to our village and recruited all the able-bodied young men to fight in the war. Because of his broken leg, my brother was spared. Our neighbors remembered my father's words; no one said anything to him."

Michael stared at his feet and didn't speak. Wei Lun waited a minute before reaching out and putting his hand on Michael's shoulder. "Listen, if you need anything, I'm right next door. You know where to find me," he said. Then he stood up and walked back to his house.

Over the next few weeks, Wei Lun continued his daily routine of gardening and working around the house. He chose not to pester his young neighbor with intrusive questions; he just nodded his head when he saw Michael and commented on the weather. Occasionally, he stopped Judy to give her a bouquet of flowers from his garden. When the two boys were out shooting baskets, he would often walk over and hand them a brown grocery bag filled with vegetables.

One day, Michael strolled into his neighbor's garden. Wei was bent over, pulling a few weeds from between his pepper plants. The old man straightened up and saw the hesitant smile on Michael's face.

"I just wanted to thank you for the vegetables and flowers. It really meant a lot to us, especially Judy. She claims I never give her flowers," said Michael with a little laugh. He continued in a more serious tone. "That story, the one about your father." Wei nodded his head. "Well, I didn't get it at first. Now, I think he might have been right. I got a new job yesterday. It's with a much smaller company, but I think I can really make a difference there. I never would have considered such a job before, never would have looked for this kind of opportunity. In a way, I'm kind of glad I was let go."

"I'm really happy to hear that you have a new job," said the old man. "When I was a boy, I never understood my father's words, either. Over the years, I've come to realize the truth in them. It's as if every prospect contains a good seed and a bad seed. You never know which will grow. Sometimes, I think it's just a matter of how we look at it."

Michael nodded his head and stretched out his hand. "Thanks for everything," he said.

Wei Lun grasped his young neighbor's hand in his still strong grip. "Good luck," he said, a broad smile crossing his face.

In Greek mythology, the Daughters of the Night, the three Fates, determined each person's lot in life. Clotho spun the thread, Lachesis measured the length of each strand while deciding individual destiny, and Atropos sheared the cord, ending a person's life. They caused both good and bad things to happen to all mortals, their formidable power a part of the natural order of things.

Today, we envision a way of life and set our goals with the expectation that our plans can be achieved—but things seldom happen quite the way we anticipate and we puzzle over the turn of events. We rejoice in our good fortune, often seeing it as a result of our own efforts. However, the difficult times, the emotional upheavals, the economic losses, the unfulfilled dreams—these we see as something much different. Our troubles are unfair, our setbacks unwarranted. We experience our lives in tiny pieces, reacting to the emotional tenor of each specific event, deeming it either good or bad.

Yet all spiritual traditions teach that good and bad occurrences are part of every life. The hard times often provide the very circumstance that guides us to unexpected insights and opens up new possibilities for growth. Time shifts and our perspective changes. It takes patience to allow time to unfold and to see how things fit together. Unexpected changes are part of life's mystery. If we lament the condition of our life, we become mired in regret. When we learn to accept our situation, we seek to understand it and work out new ways of responding. In this way, we exert some measure of control over our destiny.

DISCUSSION GUIDE

As the characters in these stories travel on their life's journey, we empathize with their trials and are able to envision the circumstances they find themselves in while we share their joys and disappointments.

Part of why we are able to relate to the characters so well is because of the universal human qualities they possess—reflections of our very own traits. Through the act of imagining we are able to place ourselves in the stories and, with little effort, imagine how we would have felt or what we would have done in their situations.

While this Discussion Guide has specific questions for each story, there are a few questions that groups can ask while they discuss *any* of the stories:

- Which character in the story do you, at least in part, resemble?

- What aspects of the character's personality that you resemble would you like to change? Which aspects do you hope will remain the same?

- Which character would you like to become?

Think of these questions as you consider the other story-specific questions. Your answers may surprise you.

A Story Not Told, a Song Not Sung

- Sharing our stories helps us connect with the people in our lives. However, there are times when people keep their stories to themselves because they do not feel anyone wants to listen. Think of a time when you tried to share a story and the listener was inattentive. Which of the feelings described in the story did you experience? What other emotions did you feel?

- Now think of a time when you told a story and the listener responded with interest and compassion. How did that make you feel? How did you respond?

- Describe what you see as the main theme of this story.

Baucis and Philemon

- What do the vivid food descriptions add to the story? Think of a time when food was part of an event in your life. In what ways did the food contribute to the environment you were in? What does it add to this story?

- Strangers often make us feel uncomfortable or fearful. Think of a time when you were a stranger. How were you made to feel welcome (or not)? What did you feel in that situation?

- Think of a time when you were in a situation to welcome someone. What happened? What about the event do you wish was different?

Catch-the-Wind

- When physical wounds heal, they can produce visible scars that are easily recognized. Imagine that you are standing next to the bell tower surrounded by sympathetic listeners. What story would you tell? What would you like your listeners to say in response to your story?

- Think of a time when someone told you about a wound or scar of their own. Would you change anything about your response? How would your response differ now?

Because I Can

- The woman who is the beggar in this story must rely on the kindness of others for survival. Imagine that you are that woman. Envision the circumstances that have caused you to beg. How does it feel to have to beg? What do you feel as a result of the disdainful faces of the men at that table? Describe the emotions you experience when the generous man heaps coins into your hand.

- Continue the story. Imagine the woman's meal that evening. What does she serve her children? What does the woman tell them? How do her children respond?

The Juggler and the Priest

- Many images in this story reveal the extraordinary marvels found in the ordinary world. Which images resonate with you? What is something simple in your life that continues to be a source of joy and wonder for you? How do you share this joy with others?

- Both the priest and the juggler, at a point in their lives, distanced themselves from the world around them. Eventually, they connected with the world through their special talents. What gifts do you possess that allow you to connect with those around you? In what ways do you connect with others?

- The priest offers the juggler a respite from his loneliness and the opportunity to discover happiness by helping others. Who in your life has enabled you to learn an important life lesson? How were these lessons taught? Who do you teach them too?

The Magic Paintbrush

- Each of us possesses talents and abilities that we can use to enrich our own life as well as the lives of those around us. Think of your talents and abilities. Is there a capability that you have not fully developed? What holds you back?

- Which of your talents are you most proud of?

- In what ways do you see people around you sharing their talents and abilities?

A Dream for Ruth

- Despite hardship, Ruth always found a way to bring beauty into her life and the lives of those around her. Explore the relationship between happiness and possessions. What is that relationship for Ruth? How about for you?

- How does Ruth's mother's ability to make a place feel like home effect Ruth?

- How do you find and create beauty in your life?

Stones and Treasures

- Imagine that you are one of the people in the crowd on the evening of the angel's visit. What burden or lament would you spit out? How has this problem shaped your life?

- How would the angel describe your trouble?

- Describe your jewel that the angel places on the tree.

Peace That Lasts

- In the opening of this story, the Buddha admonishes the monks and advises them not to cling to thoughts of past harm. Think of a time when you held a grudge. What was the result? What, if anything, did you gain? What, if anything, did you lose?

- What are your thoughts on Dighiti's advice to "Be not short-sighted. Be not long-sighted. Hatred is not quenched by hatred; hatred is only appeased by love"? In what situation can you apply this motto in your own life? How about beyond your life? Can you think of a circumstance which could benefit from having these words applied to it?

The Rich Man and the Shoemaker

- The characters in this story evoke strong feelings. Toward which character do you feel the most sympathetic? Do you identify with any one character in particular?

- The revelation of the true nature of the rich man surprises the rabbi and alters his perception of the rich man. Imagine that you are one of the people in the village who learns that the despised rich man has helped you. How would you feel? What would you say?

- Does this story remind you of anything that has happened in your own life? Describe that situation.

- While this story has many themes, describe the one that is most obvious to you. Now describe one that seems more subtle. How are these themes related? How are they different? In what ways does developing a theme for the story alter your under-standing of it?

The Spirit of the Rice Fields

- Batara Guru expresses his desire to protect Tisna Wati through both fear and anger. Explore the relationship between fear and anger. Think of a time in your life when fear or anger, or both, caused you to act impulsively. In what ways were you like Batara Guru? How were you different?

• Imagine a different ending for this story. In the new version, what would be different? What is gained from that change? What is lost?

The Squire's Party

• The fashion, cosmetic, and advertising industries spend huge amounts of time and billions of dollars to convince us of the importance of appearances. How prevalent is the concern with appearances in this story?

• Explore the relationship between perception of ourselves and how others perceive us. How is the way Patrick reacted to the treatment he received when he arrived at the party the first time, different from the way you might have reacted in the same situation?

• Add more details to the story. How do you think the squire responded to Patrick's comments at the end of the story? What did the rest of the partygoers think?

Daniel's Legacy

• Which of the characters in this story remind you of someone in your life? What qualities do you admire in that person?

• There are many poignant encounters between the characters in this story. What feelings do these meetings evoke? When Simon finds Daniel? When Daniel and Lila are reunited? When Daniel meets Samuel?

• Imagine that you are returning to your home after having been away for a long time. What are the things you would miss the most? Who would you like to see waiting for you?

• Imagine you are Lila. How would this experience have changed you?

The Junkyard Refuge

• Discuss the images of sharing. What types of sharing do you see?

• What purposes do the character of the white-haired lady serve? What does Will learn from her? What can you?

• Sanctuary is an important theme in this story. We often seek the shelter of special friends or places in times of difficulty. Think of a place that has offered you retreat in a time of struggle. What made it special?

• Describe a friend you turn to when you have problems. Which of their qualities eases your burden?

The Gift

• Which character in this story are you most like? Who are you least like?

• The farmer is able to see extraordinary beauty in ordinary things, even a simple apple. If you found a treasure of this kind, with whom would you share it? What qualities does that person possess which make you want to share your treasure with them?

• What is something ordinary that you find beauty in? What do you gain by sharing it with others?

• In what ways do you take the time to appreciate life's simple blessings? If you don't, how could you?

A Mother's Quest

• The mother in this story receives help and guidance from many people. Which of the helpers do you find most comforting? What about that character appeals to you?

• Describe your ideal guide. What characteristics would they possess? What would they look like? Who in your life is like this character?

• Describe the characteristics of the many guides and helpers in this story. What similarities do you notice? How does this observation contribute to your interpretation of the story?

The Miser

• The miser keeps his gold hidden and chooses not to use it or share it with anyone else. Which of your treasures, perhaps your time, talent, or stories, do you keep hidden? Why?

• Think of a time when you shared a piece of your treasure with someone else. What did you gain from this experience? How did you feel?

• What advice would you give the miser if you met him before all his gold was stolen? What would you say to him after it was gone?

Mary McPhee and the Pooka

• Much of the charm of this story lies in its magical images. Imagine a magical adventure of your own. Would you fly into the air? Swim to the bottom of the ocean? Burrow beneath the roots of a great tree? Find hidden treasure?

• What is the theme of your adventure? What do you discover? Do you find hope at the top of a mountain? Peace on the ocean's floor?

• What does Mary find as a result of her encounter with the Pooka?

This Too Shall Pass

• The ruler in this story searches for a guiding principle to help him achieve balance in his life, dismissing several elaborate suggestions in favor of a simple motto. What sources in your life provide direction and guidance?

• What simple motto do you live by?

• If you don't have a motto, think of one that summarizes how you live your life. In what ways is your motto helpful? How could changing it alter your outlook?

A Neighbor's Wisdom

• In this story, Wei Liang says, "It's as if every prospect contains a good seed and a bad seed. You never know which will grow. Sometimes, I think it's just a matter of how we look at it." Think of a difficult time or event in your life. Can you describe anything positive that came out of that experience? What did you learn?

• In what ways have your responses to seemingly negative situations been like Michael's when he first lost his job?

ACKNOWLEDGMENTS

I am grateful for the gift of story that graces my life in countless ways and continues to illuminate my path as I travel through life's journey.

The act of storymaking in my life is sustained by many wonderful and loving relationships that have inspired and encouraged all my creative endeavors, including this book.

I am deeply indebted to my editor, Maura Shaw, who proposed the idea for this book; to Jessica Swift, assistant editor, who carefully read the manuscript; to Stuart M. Matlins, publisher; and the entire team at SkyLight Paths Publishing, who created a wonderful opportunity for me to explore stories in a new way.

I would like to honor the memory of my father, Stuart Hartin; and my uncles Milton, Clifford, and Beattie Hartin; Albert and Allan Lowe; and Joe and Gerald MacGillis. I can still hear the echo of their voices as they shared their stories. It was from them that I learned how sweet the human voice could be.

I am thankful for the community of storytellers around the country who nurture and inspire my work as a storyteller. Within that community, I have discovered a circle of friends who nourish my spirit and teach me how to live. I want to thank Tracy Leavitt for bringing Visions Story and Art Center to the Hudson Valley and for giving me a chance to tell stories. Mary B. Summerlin has patiently listened to many personal stories and given me the encouragement I needed to share them. I genuinely appreciate the generosity of Muriel Horowitz, who steadfastly combines her faith, her Jewish stories, and her life into a seamless garment. Jack Maguire has kindly shared his wisdom and shown me what truly lies at the heart of storytelling. Joanne Renbeck fosters my artistic sensibilities and helps me see the beauty in life. Karen Pillsworth has given me the truest example of friendship I have ever known and continues to accompany me on one story adventure after another.

I want to thank my mother, Ann Hartin, for her gentle support and continuous prayers. I cannot imagine my life without my brothers, Douglas and Bryan Hartin, and my sister, Maggie Reilly. They have stood by me in my darkest moments and are the heroes of my story.

My children, Meghan, Kevin, and Brendan, fill my days with love and are a continuous source of delight in my life as I watch their stories unfold.

Finally, I want to thank my husband, David, for his love and support throughout this project. May we continue to treasure each other's stories.

SOURCE NOTES

Most of the stories in this collection have been told since long ago in many versions, in many languages, in many cultures. I have told them again in new versions here, adapted to my own voice.

Chapter 1: A Story Not Told, a Song Not Sung

I first heard a version of this story from Letty Umidi. I adapted my version from "The Story Not Told, the Song Not Sung" in *Three Minute Tales: Stories from Around the World to Tell or Read When Time Is Short,* by Margaret Read MacDonald (Little Rock, Ark.: August House Publishers, 2004), pp. 75–76.

Chapter 2: Baucis and Philemon

I relied on several versions of this well-known tale, including "Baucis and Philemon" in *Tales the Muses Told,* selected and related by Roger Lancelyn Green (New York: Henry Z. Walck, 1965), pp. 37–42.

Chapter 3: Catch-the-Wind

This story was inspired by "Catch-the-Wind" from *Baba Yaga's Geese and Other Russian Stories,* translated and adapted by Bonnie Carey (Bloomington: Indiana University Press, 1973), 27–32.

Chapter 4: Because I Can

This story was inspired by "Know Yourself: A Tale from the Middle East," in *Ayat Jamilah: Beautiful Signs—A Treasury of Islamic Wisdom for Children and Parents,* by Sarah Conover and Freda Crane (Spokane: Eastern Washington University Press, 2004), pp. 96–97.

Chapter 5: The Juggler and the Priest

I have read many versions of this tale, most notably "The Clown of God" from *The Christmas Book of Legends and Stories,* by Elva Sophronia Smith and Alice Isabel Hazeltine (New York: Lothrop & Lee, 1944), pp. 311–20.

Chapter 6: The Magic Paintbrush

This is a well-known folktale in China and I have read many versions of it. I was inspired by "Ma Liang" in *Traditional Chinese Folktales,* edited by Yin-lien C. Chin, Yetta S. Center, and Mildred Ross (Armonk, N.Y.: M. E. Sharpe, 1989), pp. 141–53; and by "How Wang-Fo Was Saved" in *Oriental Tales,* by Marguerite Yourcenar, translated from the French by Alberto Manguel, in collaboration with the author (New York: The Noonday Press/Farrar Straus Giroux, 1983), pp. 3–20.

Chapter 7: A Dream for Ruth

This story was inspired by Elizabeth Ellis's version of "The Pedlar of Swaffham" entitled "The Peddlar's Dream" found in *Homespun: Tales From America's Favorite Storytellers,* edited by Jimmy Neil Smith (New York: Crown Publishers, 1988) pp. 20–22.

Chapter 8: Stones and Treasures

I have read and heard several versions of this story, including "The Ragged Pedlar" in *My Book House,* edited by Olive Beaupre Miller (Lake Bluff, Ill.: Book House for Children, 1960), pp. 252–56.

Chapter 9: Peace That Lasts

I read many versions of this tale, including "Brahmadatta, Dighiti and Dighavu" in *Buddhist Parables,* translated from the original Pali by Eugene Watson Burlingame (New Haven, Conn.: Yale University Press, 1922), pp. 20–29.

Chapter 10: The Rich Man and the Shoemaker

I was inspired by a tale found in *Folktales of Israel,* edited by Dov Noy with Dan Ben Amos (Chicago: University of Chicago Press, 1963), pp. 11–12.

Chapter 11: The Spirit of the Rice Fields

I have read many versions of this tale, including "The Soul of the Mountain Rice" in *Indonesian Legends and Folktales,* by Adele de Leeuw (Edinburgh, N.Y.: Nelson, 1961), pp. 21–24.

Chapter 12: The Squire's Party

I heard several versions of this tale during a Visions Story Circle story swap, including one from Jonathan Heiles where the main character was Nasreddin Hodja, a well-known trickster-hero from the Middle East, and another from Muriel Horowitz in which the main character is Elijah the Prophet, from Jewish folklore.

Chapter 13: Daniel's Legacy

This story is my retelling of "The Cow-Tail Switch" from *The Cow-Tail Switch and Other West African Tales,* by Harold Courlander and George Herzog (New York: Henry Holt, 1974), 5–12.

Chapter 14: The Junkyard Refuge

This tale was inspired by "The Magic Garden" in *Stories of the Steppes: Kazakh Folktales,* by Mary Lou Masey (New York: David McKay, 1968), 50–61. Also, "The Magic Garden of the Poor" from *Earth Care: World Folktales to Talk About,* by Margaret Read MacDonald (North Haven, Conn.: Linnet Books, 1999), 129–37.

Chapter 15: The Gift

I adapted this tale from "The Gift and the Giver" in *The Lion's Whiskers: Tales of High Africa,* by Russell Davis and Brent Ashabranner (Boston: Little & Brown, 1959), pp. 172–77.

Chapter 16: A Mother's Quest

I adapted this tale from "The Stolen Bairn and the Sidhe," by Sorche Nic Leodhas, in *Thistle and Thyme, Tales and Legends from Scotland* (New York: Holt, Rinehart and Winston, 1962), pp. 46–61.

Chapter 17: The Miser

This is a well-known tale from Aesop, which I remember from my childhood. A version can be found in *Aesop's Fables,* by Jerry Pinkney (New York: SeaStar Books, 2000), p. 32.

Chapter 18: Mary McPhee and the Pooka

I heard this story, a version of the well-known "The Hedley Kow," from my friend, Jane Gregory, one evening as we drove through the Pennsylvania landscape on a summer's eve, looking for the site of a storytelling conference.

Chapter 19: This Too Shall Pass

This story was inspired by "The Lesson of the Man in the Felt Cap" from *Attar: Stories for Young Adults,* translated and adapted from the Persian by Muhammad Nur Abdus Salam (ABC International Group, 2000), pp. 149–55.

Chapter 20: A Neighbor's Wisdom

This is a tale within a tale. The frame of this story was inspired by "That Is Good" from *Doorways to the Soul,* by Elisa Davy Pearmain (Cleveland: The Pilgrim Press, 1998), pp. 5–6. The inner story is one of several versions that I heard during a Visions Story Circle story swap.

Bible Fiction / Folktales

Abraham's Bind & Other Bible Tales of Trickery, Folly, Mercy and Love *by Michael J. Caduto*

New retellings of episodes in the lives of familiar biblical characters explore relevant life lessons.

6 x 9, 224 pp, HC, 978-1-59473-186-0 **$19.99**

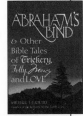

Daughters of the Desert: Stories of Remarkable Women from Christian, Jewish and Muslim Traditions *by Claire Rudolf Murphy, Meghan Nuttall Sayres, Mary Cronk Farrell, Sarah Conover and Betsy Wharton*

Breathes new life into the old tales of our female ancestors in faith. Uses traditional scriptural passages as starting points, then with vivid detail fills in historical context and place. Chapters reveal the voices of Sarah, Hagar, Huldah, Esther, Salome, Mary Magdalene, Lydia, Khadija, Fatima and many more. Historical fiction ideal for readers of all ages. Quality paperback includes reader's discussion guide.

5½ x 8½, 192 pp, Quality PB, 978-1-59473-106-8 **$14.99**
HC, 192 pp, 978-1-893361-72-0 **$19.95**

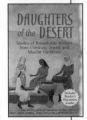

The Triumph of Eve & Other Subversive Bible Tales
by Matt Biers-Ariel

Many people were taught and remember only a one-dimensional Bible. These engaging retellings are the antidote to this—they're witty, often hilarious, always profound, and invite you to grapple with questions and issues that are often hidden in the original text.

5½ x 8½, 192 pp, HC, 978-1-59473-040-5 **$19.99**

Also avail.: The Triumph of Eve Teacher's Guide
8½ x 11, 44 pp, PB, 978-1-59473-152-5 **$8.99**

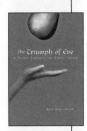

Religious Etiquette / Reference

How to Be a Perfect Stranger, 4th Edition: The Essential Religious Etiquette Handbook *Edited by Stuart M. Matlins and Arthur J. Magida*

The indispensable guidebook to help the well-meaning guest when visiting other people's religious ceremonies. A straightforward guide to the rituals and celebrations of the major religions and denominations in the United States and Canada from the perspective of an interested guest of any other faith, based on information obtained from authorities of each religion. Belongs in every living room, library and office. Covers:

African American Methodist Churches • Assemblies of God • Bahá'í • Baptist • Buddhist • Christian Church (Disciples of Christ) • Christian Science (Church of Christ, Scientist) • Churches of Christ • Episcopalian and Anglican • Hindu • Islam • Jehovah's Witnesses • Jewish • Lutheran • Mennonite/Amish • Methodist • Mormon (Church of Jesus Christ of Latter-day Saints) • Native American/First Nations • Orthodox Churches • Pentecostal Church of God • Presbyterian • Quaker (Religious Society of Friends) • Reformed Church in America/Canada • Roman Catholic • Seventh-day Adventist • Sikh • Unitarian Universalist • United Church of Canada • United Church of Christ

6 x 9, 432 pp, Quality PB, 978-1-59473-140-2 **$19.99**

Or phone, fax, mail or e-mail to: SKYLIGHT PATHS Publishing
Sunset Farm Offices, Route 4 • P.O. Box 237 • Woodstock, Vermont 05091
Tel: (802) 457-4000 • Fax: (802) 457-4004 • www.skylightpaths.com
Credit card orders: (800) 962-4544 (8:30AM–5:30PM ET Monday–Friday)
Generous discounts on quantity orders. SATISFACTION GUARANTEED. Prices subject to change.

Sacred Texts—SkyLight Illuminations Series
Andrew Harvey, Series Editor

Offers today's spiritual seeker an accessible entry into the great classic texts of the world's spiritual traditions. Each classic is presented in an accessible translation, with facing pages of guided commentary from experts, giving you the keys you need to understand the history, context and meaning of the text. This series enables you, whatever your background, to experience and understand classic spiritual texts directly, and to make them a part of your life.

CHRISTIANITY

The End of Days: Essential Selections from Apocalyptic Texts—
Annotated & Explained *Annotation by Robert G. Clouse*
Introduces you to the beliefs and values held by those who rely on the promises found in the Book of Revelation. 5½ x 8½, 192 pp, Quality PB, 978-1-59473-170-9 **$16.99**

The Hidden Gospel of Matthew: Annotated & Explained
Translation & Annotation by Ron Miller
Takes you deep into the text cherished around the world to discover the words and events that have the strongest connection to the historical Jesus.
5½ x 8½, 272 pp, Quality PB, 978-1-59473-038-2 **$16.99**

The Lost Sayings of Jesus: Teachings from Ancient Christian, Jewish, Gnostic and Islamic Sources—Annotated & Explained
Translation & Annotation by Andrew Phillip Smith; Foreword by Stephan A. Hoeller
This collection of more than three hundred sayings depicts Jesus as a Wisdom teacher who speaks to people of all faiths as a mystic and spiritual master.
5½ x 8½, 240 pp, Quality PB, 978-1-59473-172-3 **$16.99**

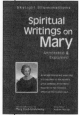

Philokalia: The Eastern Christian Spiritual Texts—Selections Annotated & Explained *Annotation by Allyne Smith; Translation by G. E. H. Palmer, Phillip Sherrard and Bishop Kallistos Ware*
The first approachable introduction to the wisdom of the Philokalia, which is the classic text of Eastern Christian spirituality.
5½ x 8½, 256 pp, Quality PB, 978-1-59473-103-7 **$16.99**

Spiritual Writings on Mary: Annotated & Explained
Annotation by Mary Ford-Grabowsky; Foreword by Andrew Harvey
Examines the role of Mary, the mother of Jesus, as a source of inspiration in history and in life today. 5½ x 8½, 288 pp, Quality PB, 978-1-59473-001-6 **$16.99**

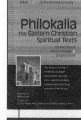

The Way of a Pilgrim: Annotated & Explained
Translation & Annotation by Gleb Pokrovsky; Foreword by Andrew Harvey
This classic of Russian spirituality is the delightful account of one man who sets out to learn the prayer of the heart, also known as the "Jesus prayer."
5½ x 8½, 160 pp, Illus., Quality PB, 978-1-893361-31-7 **$14.95**

MORMONISM

The Book of Mormon: Selections Annotated & Explained
Annotation by Jana Riess; Foreword by Phyllis Tickle
Explores the sacred epic that is cherished by more than twelve million members of the LDS church as the keystone of their faith.
5½ x 8½ , 272 pp, Quality PB, 978-1-59473-076-4 **$16.99**

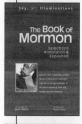

NATIVE AMERICAN

Native American Stories of the Sacred: Annotated & Explained
Retold & Annotated by Evan T. Pritchard
Intended for more than entertainment, these teaching tales contain elegantly simple illustrations of time-honored truths.
5½ x 8½, 272 pp, Quality PB, 978-1-59473-112-9 **$16.99**

Sacred Texts—cont.

GNOSTICISM

The Gospel of Philip: Annotated & Explained
Translation & Annotation by Andrew Phillip Smith; Foreword by Stevan Davies
Reveals otherwise unrecorded sayings of Jesus and fragments of Gnostic mythology.
5½ x 8½, 160 pp, Quality PB, 978-1-59473-111-2 **$16.99**

The Gospel of Thomas: Annotated & Explained
Translation & Annotation by Stevan Davies Sheds new light on the origins of Christianity and portrays Jesus as a wisdom-loving sage. 5½ x 8½, 192 pp, Quality PB, 978-1-893361-45-4 **$16.99**

The Secret Book of John: The Gnostic Gospel—Annotated & Explained
Translation & Annotation by Stevan Davies The most significant and influential text of the ancient Gnostic religion. 5½ x 8½, 208 pp, Quality PB, 978-1-59473-082-5 **$16.99**

JUDAISM

The Divine Feminine in Biblical Wisdom Literature
Selections Annotated & Explained
Translation & Annotation by Rabbi Rami Shapiro; Foreword by Rev. Cynthia Bourgeault, PhD
Uses the Hebrew books of Psalms, Proverbs, Song of Songs, Ecclesiastes and Job, Wisdom literature and the Wisdom of Solomon to clarify who Wisdom is.
5½ x 8½, 240 pp, Quality PB, 978-1-59473-109-9 **$16.99**

Ethics of the Sages: *Pirke Avot*—Annotated & Explained
Translation & Annotation by Rabbi Rami Shapiro Clarifies the ethical teachings of the early Rabbis. 5½ x 8½, 192 pp, Quality PB, 978-1-59473-207-2 **$16.99**

Hasidic Tales: Annotated & Explained
Translation & Annotation by Rabbi Rami Shapiro
Introduces the legendary tales of the impassioned Hasidic rabbis, presenting them as stories rather than as parables. 5½ x 8½, 240 pp, Quality PB, 978-1-893361-86-7 **$16.95**

The Hebrew Prophets: Selections Annotated & Explained
Translation & Annotation by Rabbi Rami Shapiro; Foreword by Zalman M. Schachter-Shalomi
Focuses on the central themes covered by all the Hebrew prophets.
5½ x 8½, 224 pp, Quality PB, 978-1-59473-037-5 **$16.99**

Zohar: Annotated & Explained *Translation & Annotation by Daniel C. Matt*
The best-selling author of *The Essential Kabbalah* brings together in one place the most important teachings of the Zohar, the canonical text of Jewish mystical tradition.
5½ x 8½, 176 pp, Quality PB, 978-1-893361-51-5 **$15.99**

EASTERN RELIGIONS

Bhagavad Gita: Annotated & Explained *Translation by Shri Purohit Swami*
Annotation by Kendra Crossen Burroughs Explains references and philosophical terms, shares the interpretations of famous spiritual leaders and scholars, and more.
5½ x 8½, 192 pp, Quality PB, 978-1-893361-28-7 **$16.95**

Dhammapada: Annotated & Explained *Translation by Max Müller and revised by Jack Maguire; Annotation by Jack Maguire* Contains all of Buddhism's key teachings.
5½ x 8½, 160 pp, b/w photos, Quality PB, 978-1-893361-42-3 **$14.95**

Rumi and Islam: Selections from His Stories, Poems, and Discourses—
Annotated & Explained *Translation & Annotation by Ibrahim Gamard*
Focuses on Rumi's place within the Sufi tradition of Islam, providing insight into the mystical side of the religion. 5½ x 8½, 240 pp, Quality PB, 978-1-59473-002-3 **$15.99**

Selections from the Gospel of Sri Ramakrishna: Annotated & Explained
Translation by Swami Nikhilananda; Annotation by Kendra Crossen Burroughs
Introduces the fascinating world of the Indian mystic and the universal appeal of his message. 5½ x 8½, 240 pp, b/w photos, Quality PB, 978-1-893361-46-1 **$16.95**

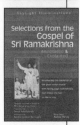

Tao Te Ching: Annotated & Explained *Translation & Annotation by Derek Lin*
Introduces an Eastern classic in an accessible, poetic and completely original way.
5½ x 8½, 192 pp, Quality PB, 978-1-59473-204-1 **$16.99**

Spirituality of the Seasons

Autumn: A Spiritual Biography of the Season
Edited by Gary Schmidt and Susan M. Felch; Illustrations by Mary Azarian
Rejoice in autumn as a time of preparation and reflection. Includes Wendell Berry, David James Duncan, Robert Frost, A. Bartlett Giamatti, E. B. White, P. D. James, Julian of Norwich, Garret Keizer, Tracy Kidder, Anne Lamott, May Sarton.
6 x 9, 320 pp, 5 b/w illus., Quality PB, 978-1-59473-118-1 **$18.99**
HC, 978-1-59473-005-4 **$22.99**

Spring: A Spiritual Biography of the Season
Edited by Gary Schmidt and Susan M. Felch; Illustrations by Mary Azarian
Explore the gentle unfurling of spring and reflect on how nature celebrates rebirth and renewal. Includes Jane Kenyon, Lucy Larcom, Harry Thurston, Nathaniel Hawthorne, Noel Perrin, Annie Dillard, Martha Ballard, Barbara Kingsolver, Dorothy Wordsworth, Donald Hall, David Brill, Lionel Basney, Isak Dinesen, Paul Laurence Dunbar.
6 x 9, 352 pp, 6 b/w illus., HC, 978-1-59473-114-3 **$21.99**

Summer: A Spiritual Biography of the Season
Edited by Gary Schmidt and Susan M. Felch; Illustrations by Barry Moser
"A sumptuous banquet.... These selections lift up an exquisite wholeness found within an everyday sophistication."— ★ *Publishers Weekly* starred review
Includes Anne Lamott, Luci Shaw, Ray Bradbury, Richard Selzer, Thomas Lynch, Walt Whitman, Carl Sandburg, Sherman Alexie, Madeleine L'Engle, Jamaica Kincaid.
6 x 9, 304 pp, 5 b/w illus., HC, 978-1-59473-083-2 **$21.99**

Winter: A Spiritual Biography of the Season
Edited by Gary Schmidt and Susan M. Felch; Illustrations by Barry Moser
"This outstanding anthology features top-flight nature and spirituality writers on the fierce, inexorable season of winter.... Remarkably lively and warm, despite the icy subject." — ★ *Publishers Weekly* starred review.
Includes Will Campbell, Rachel Carson, Annie Dillard, Donald Hall, Ron Hansen, Jane Kenyon, Jamaica Kincaid, Barry Lopez, Kathleen Norris, John Updike, E. B. White.
6 x 9, 288 pp, 6 b/w illus., Deluxe PB w/flaps, 978-1-893361-92-8 **$18.95**
HC, 978-1-893361-53-9 **$21.95**

Spirituality / Animal Companions

Blessing the Animals: Prayers and Ceremonies to Celebrate God's Creatures, Wild and Tame *Edited by Lynn L. Caruso* 5 x 7¼, 256 pp, HC, 978-1-59473-145-7 **$19.99**

What Animals Can Teach Us about Spirituality: Inspiring Lessons from Wild and Tame Creatures *by Diana L. Guerrero* 6 x 9, 176 pp, Quality PB, 978-1-893361-84-3 **$16.95**

Spirituality

Awakening the Spirit, Inspiring the Soul
30 Stories of Interspiritual Discovery in the Community of Faiths
Edited by Brother Wayne Teasdale and Martha Howard, MD; Foreword by Joan Borysenko, PhD
Thirty original spiritual mini-autobiographies showcase the varied ways that people come to faith—and what that means—in today's multi-religious world.
6 x 9, 224 pp, HC, 978-1-59473-039-9 **$21.99**

The Alphabet of Paradise: An A–Z of Spirituality for Everyday Life
by Howard Cooper 5 x 7¼, 224 pp, Quality PB, 978-1-893361-80-5 **$16.95**

Creating a Spiritual Retirement: A Guide to the Unseen Possibilities in Our Lives
by Molly Srode 6 x 9, 208 pp, b/w photos, Quality PB, 978-1-59473-050-4 **$14.99**
HC, 978-1-893361-75-1 **$19.95**

Finding Hope: Cultivating God's Gift of a Hopeful Spirit
by Marcia Ford 8 x 8, 200 pp, Quality PB, 978-1-59473-211-9 **$16.99**

The Geography of Faith: Underground Conversations on Religious, Political and Social Change *by Daniel Berrigan and Robert Coles* 6 x 9, 224 pp, Quality PB, 978-1-893361-40-9 **$16.95**

God Within: Our Spiritual Future—As Told by Today's New Adults *Edited by Jon M. Sweeney and the Editors at SkyLight Paths* 6 x 9, 176 pp, Quality PB, 978-1-893361-15-7 **$14.95**

Spirituality & Crafts

The Knitting Way: A Guide to Spiritual Self-Discovery
by Linda Skolnik and Janice MacDaniels
7 x 9, 240 pp, Quality PB, 978-1-59473-079-5 **$16.99**

The Quilting Path
A Guide to Spiritual Discovery through Fabric, Thread and Kabbalah
by Louise Silk
7 x 9, 192 pp, Quality PB, 978-1-59473-206-5 **$16.99**

Spiritual Practice

Divining the Body
Reclaim the Holiness of Your Physical Self *by Jan Phillips*
A practical and inspiring guidebook for connecting the body and soul in spiritual practice. Leads you into a milieu of reverence, mystery and delight, helping you discover your body as a pathway to the Divine.
8 x 8, 256 pp, Quality PB, 978-1-59473-080-1 **$16.99**

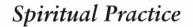

Finding Time for the Timeless: Spirituality in the Workweek
by John McQuiston II
Simple, refreshing stories that provide you with examples of how you can refocus and enrich your daily life using prayer or meditation, ritual and other forms of spiritual practice. 5½ x 6¾, 208 pp, HC, 978-1-59473-035-1 **$17.99**

The Gospel of Thomas
A Guidebook for Spiritual Practice *by Ron Miller; Translations by Stevan Davies*
An innovative guide to bring a new spiritual classic into daily life.
6 x 9, 160 pp, Quality PB, 978-1-59473-047-4 **$14.99**

Earth, Water, Fire, and Air: Essential Ways of Connecting to Spirit
by Cait Johnson 6 x 9, 224 pp, HC, 978-1-893361-65-2 **$19.95**

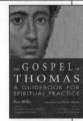

Labyrinths from the Outside In: Walking to Spiritual Insight—A Beginner's Guide
by Donna Schaper and Carole Ann Camp
6 x 9, 208 pp, b/w illus. and photos, Quality PB, 978-1-893361-18-8 **$16.95**

Practicing the Sacred Art of Listening: A Guide to Enrich Your Relationships
and Kindle Your Spiritual Life—The Listening Center Workshop
by Kay Lindahl 8 x 8, 176 pp, Quality PB, 978-1-893361-85-0 **$16.95**

Releasing the Creative Spirit: Unleash the Creativity in Your Life
by Dan Wakefield 7 x 10, 256 pp, Quality PB, 978-1-893361-36-2 **$16.95**

The Sacred Art of Bowing: Preparing to Practice
by Andi Young 5½ x 8½, 128 pp, b/w illus., Quality PB, 978-1-893361-82-9 **$14.95**

The Sacred Art of Chant: Preparing to Practice
by Ana Hernández 5½ x 8½, 192 pp, Quality PB, 978-1-59473-036-8 **$15.99**

The Sacred Art of Fasting: Preparing to Practice
by Thomas Ryan, CSP 5½ x 8½, 192 pp, Quality PB, 978-1-59473-078-8 **$15.99**

The Sacred Art of Forgiveness: Forgiving Ourselves and Others through God's Grace
by Marcia Ford 8 x 8, 176 pp, Quality PB, 978-1-59473-175-4 **$16.99**

The Sacred Art of Listening: Forty Reflections for Cultivating a Spiritual Practice
by Kay Lindahl; Illustrations by Amy Schnapper
8 x 8, 160 pp, b/w illus., Quality PB, 978-1-893361-44-7 **$16.99**

The Sacred Art of Lovingkindness: Preparing to Practice
by Rabbi Rami Shapiro; Foreword by Marcia Ford
5½ x 8½, 176 pp, Quality PB, 978-1-59473-151-8 **$16.99**

Sacred Speech: A Practical Guide for Keeping Spirit in Your Speech
by Rev. Donna Schaper 6 x 9, 176 pp, Quality PB, 978-1-59473-068-9 **$15.99**
HC, 978-1-893361-74-4 **$21.95**